Pandas
on the Eastside

Pandas
on the Eastside

Gabrielle Prendergast

ORCA BOOK PUBLISHERS

Text copyright © 2016 Gabrielle Prendergast

Library and Archives Canada Cataloguing in Publication

Prendergast, Gabrielle, author
Pandas on the eastside / Gabrielle Prendergast.

Issued in print and electronic formats.
ISBN 978-1-4598-1143-0 (paperback).—ISBN 978-1-4598-1144-7 (pdf).—
ISBN 978-1-4598-1145-4 (epub)

I. Title.
PS8631.R448P35 2016   jC813'.6   C2016-900530-5
                             C2016-900531-3

First published in the United States, 2016
Library of Congress Control Number: 2016931890

Summary: In this middle-grade novel set in 1973, ten-year-old Journey rallies her friends and neighbors to come to the aid of two stranded pandas.

Orca Book Publishers is dedicated to preserving the environment and has printed this book on Forest Stewardship Council® certified paper.

Orca Book Publishers gratefully acknowledges the support for its publishing programs provided by the following agencies: the Government of Canada through the Canada Book Fund and the Canada Council for the Arts, and the Province of British Columbia through the BC Arts Council and the Book Publishing Tax Credit.

Cover artwork by Taryn Gee
Author photo by Leonard Layton

ORCA BOOK PUBLISHERS
www.orcabook.com

Printed and bound in Canada.

19 18 17 16 • 4 3 2 1

For Lucy

One
Journey Wind Song

My neighborhood, the Eastside, is about the unlike-liest place on earth you would ever think to see a panda. But life is full of surprises.

Some people call the Eastside a slum. That's because they are describing buildings and roads instead of people. To them, people on the Eastside probably look poor, sad, uneducated, sick and worthless. But I don't care what they think. To me, the people around here are friends. Kellie Rae on the corner, who Mom tells me to ignore? She gives me dimes to buy Popsicles. Those guys who sell stuff I'm not allowed to even see, much less think about buying? They call me Singalong, let me take their pop bottles back and get snippy when their customers litter. And Kentucky Jack, Contrary Gary and the rest, who sleep on the street until well into winter? If it weren't for them, I wouldn't know any swearwords at all. And I think a girl called Journey might need high-quality swearwords one day.

That's right, Journey is my name. Journey Wind Song. That's pretty much all I know for sure about myself. Mom sometimes says I'm part Viking, but Kentucky Jack, who has never, by the way, been anywhere near Kentucky, says I look just like his cousin's girlfriend, and she's *pure Indian through and through and never been off the rez*. Kellie Rae always says *Aloha* to me and tells me I must be a Hawaiian princess or something. Mom has red hair and freckles, so obviously there was something going on with my dad that gave me the black hair, but this is one of the things Mom never talks about.

Mom tells me all kinds of other stuff I'm sure I don't need to know. She tells me about the war, and about the prime minister and his pretty wife, and about all the weird ingredients in orange soda. But she never tells me anything about my dad.

All I ever get is this speech: *He didn't stick around after you were born. That's all you need to know.* Why would I need to know about the ingredients in orange soda but not need to know anything about my own father? I think when Mom says, *That's all you need to know,* what she really means is "That's all I want to tell you." There's a difference. But Mom doesn't see it that way.

The past is gone, she says, as though it's a book I left on the bus and should just forget about. But how can I forget a past I never knew anything about in the first place?

Sometimes, when she's slipped a little and smells of wine, she lies on the sofa and calls me Scheherazade. I asked my teacher what that meant and she gave me a book called *The Arabian Nights,* so I don't know—maybe I'm an Arab. I don't look like any of the girls from *The Brady Bunch* or like any doll, that's for sure.

Mom says she was one of the first people to give a kid a name like Journey Wind. Nowadays you can't walk down the street without tripping over a baby named Rainbow or Sunshine or a toddler called Freedom or Phoenix. But most girls my age are called Mary or Julie or Nancy or Jackie. Jackie was the name of the president's wife the year I was born, 1962. So there are a lot of Jackies, but not too many Journeys in grade five at Eastside Elementary. Mom was a real trailblazer, an innovator namewise. She says she was a hippie before anyone even knew there were hippies. She calls herself Heather some days. On others, she goes by Bird. Bird Song. Get it?

Song is not our real last name. I found my birth certificate one day when I was looking for a quarter to buy milk. My real first name is Journey and my real middle name is Wind, but my last name is actually Flanagan, which is about as far from Song as you can get. And it's sure not a Viking name. Under *Father* it says *Unknown*.

So I go by Journey Song. That's what I write on my schoolbooks anyway. My school is three blocks from our apartment, and in the morning I sometimes have to step over puddles of pee or worse things, but mostly the streets are quiet at that time. All the kids at school live on the Eastside. No one from the outside would ever send their kid to an

Eastside school. Some kids at school don't even speak English. Some kids never bring lunch. Some kids only come to class once or twice a week, or they come late every day. My teacher, Miss Bickerstaff, sighs a lot and sends a lot of notes home and writes letters to politicians. I've heard some parents' gossip in the schoolyard that all she wants is more pay and better sofas in the staff room, but she let me read one of the letters once. She was asking for more books and chalk and better blackboards. Stuff for us, not her. Stuff to make the school a better place to learn. *Learning is the key that unlocks your future, Journey*, she said. Then she blew her nose. Our classroom is real dusty sometimes.

I think it must be hard to be a teacher on the Eastside.

Two
Miss Bickerstaff

I saw the headline on a piece of newspaper that Kentucky Jack had folded over his head to keep the morning sun out of his eyes while he slept in the bus shelter.

"Ewwww!" Nancy Pendleton said when I leaned down to take a closer look.

I could hear Jack snoring under the newspaper, and I could sure smell him too, but I wanted to read the headline. *PANDAS COMING TO AMERICA.* Under the paper, Jack grunted and rolled over in his sleep. The newspaper slipped off his head and fell into a suspicious-looking puddle under the bench.

"Gross! Don't pick it up!" Nancy said. I really

wanted to, but she was probably right. Who knew what was in that puddle?

"There are pandas coming to America," I said as we walked away.

"What are pandas?" Nancy said. Nancy was one of the kids at our school who never really learned to read. It wasn't her fault. She has something wrong with her eyes that makes the letters look upside down and backward, and the words get all mixed up. I tried to explain it to a teacher, Mrs. Parker, one day when we were in grade two, but she made us both write lines on the board. *I will not tell lies*, we wrote twenty times. Most of Nancy's lines said *I llw ont tle lise*. Teachers never made Nancy write lines again. But they never taught her to read either.

"A panda is a bear. It's mostly white, with black eyes," I explained.

"Black eyes?" Nancy said. "Did someone punch them?"

"No," I explained patiently. "They just have black fur around their eyes. Like raccoons. They come from China."

"From China? And they're coming to America? Are they going to swim?"

I really wanted to laugh then, because the idea of pandas swimming across the Pacific Ocean was sure funny, but Nancy had a habit of body checking people who laugh at her.

"I think they'll probably come in a boat," I said. "I sure wish I could see a panda. That would be groovy." *Groovy* was a word I heard the big kids saying all the time. I liked the way it sounded, like the purr of a big fluffy cat. *Groooooooovvvvvyyyy.*

"Maybe you can see one," Nancy said. "When they get to America, where will they go?"

"Washington, DC, it said. That's the far Washington, not the close one."

Nancy looked disappointed. But even if the pandas were going to the close Washington, that was still hours away, and anyway, I could never afford to go. And certainly Nancy couldn't.

"Maybe there will be a picture in the paper when they arrive," I said. Then I made a promise to myself to save up a few dimes so if there *was* a picture in the paper, I could buy a copy instead of picking a greasy one out of the trash. I would put the picture of the pandas on my wall, next to the ones my mom gave me of the moon landing and Martin Luther King and the helicopter taking off from that big concert in the field with the funny name.

When we got to school I wanted to tell everyone about the pandas, but Miss Bickerstaff was crying in the hallway outside our room. The principal, Mr. Hartnell, and the secretary, Mrs. Bent, were holding her. Then she fell down on her knees, and Mrs. Bent went down with her. Her knees hitting the hard wood floor made me get a pain in my stomach, but she didn't wince or anything—she just held on to Miss Bickerstaff even tighter.

"Get the children into the classroom," Mrs. Bent said to Mr. Hartnell, like she was the principal and he worked for her. But he did what she said.

"Don't just stand around like dazed sheep—get into the classroom," he said to me and the other kids who were watching poor Miss Bickerstaff sob on the floor. Even though I'd seen people arrested or taken away in ambulances, I thought Miss Bickerstaff on the floor was about the worst thing I'd ever seen.

We all walked into class, quiet and shocked, and sat down at our desks in the most orderly fashion ever. Mr. Hartnell looked at us for a long time, frowning.

"I imagine Miss Bickerstaff will be going home for today," he said finally.

A couple of kids just nodded.

"She's had some bad news." He stopped and looked out the window. "You know about the war, right?"

"In Vietnam?" I said after a few silent seconds had gone past.

"Miss Bickerstaff's brother was fighting in the war and…"

"He died?" I said. I knew Miss Bickerstaff's brother was in the war. She had a picture of him in his uniform in her drawer. I'd seen it when I got a paper clip for my book report. Miss Bickerstaff's brother was only nineteen years old.

"Yes. He died," Mr. Hartnell said. He didn't act surprised that I had guessed it. "The army told his mother, and she called the school. Asked me to tell Miss Bickerstaff. So I did."

Behind me I could hear Nancy and Michael Booker, who by some miracle had come to class on time, begin to fidget.

"I'm going to get the projector and see what films are in the library. Maybe there's something from *National Geographic*." He turned to the door. "You can watch something until I can get a substitute." Normally this would have made the whole class cheer, but we all just sat there like dolls on a shelf. "Journey, you're in charge," Mr. Hartnell said as he left.

I turned around to look at my classmates, fully expecting them to start making spitballs and throwing paper airplanes, but nobody moved. Then the door opened and Miss Bickerstaff came in, with Mrs. Bent still holding on to her.

"She just needs her purse," Mrs. Bent said.

Please don't let it be in the drawer, I said to myself. Please let her purse be anywhere else. But she reached down and opened the drawer. Then she froze. Every part of her froze. Except her face. Her face kind of folded up, and she closed her eyes. Mrs. Bent clung to her, and they just stood there while Miss Bickerstaff shook with sobs.

Then a miracle happened.

Nancy started to sing. Now Nancy might have been kind of slow sometimes, and she couldn't read a word, but she could sing like an angel sent from God. Who knows how she learned the words to any songs, because her family was too poor to have a stereo, and her older brother was always hogging the radio to listen to hockey or baseball, and Nancy for sure never went to church. But somehow, some way, she started singing "Amazing Grace." It was like that song came right out of Miss Bickerstaff's heart and into Nancy's, and then Nancy sang it out so we could all understand what Miss Bickerstaff was going through.

After Nancy had sung two lines, Michael joined in. Then Patty Maguire started. Jen Chow, who could barely speak English, sang too, and she sang the words more clearly than she has ever spoken. Anjali sang, even though she believes in a whole other god, and David Schuman sang, even though he doesn't believe in God at all because his parents are communists. Soon everyone was singing. I knew the song. Finally I couldn't hold my mouth closed anymore.

Even though I always think I sing like a frog, I opened up, and the sound that came out was like a ringing bell, clear and pretty and sad.

We sang that song all the way through, and when we finished, Miss Bickerstaff opened her eyes, reached down and pulled her purse and the photograph out of the drawer, closed the drawer slowly and stood up, hugging both things to her chest. She wasn't crying anymore, although Mrs. Bent sure was. They didn't say anything. They just walked out of the classroom, holding on to each other.

A long time went by. No one said or did anything. When I turned back to look at Nancy, she had fallen asleep on her desk.

Nancy is like that.

Three
Nancy Pendleton

Nancy Pendleton has been my best friend since kindergarten, when she poured a whole cup of Tang over the head of Michael Booker because he pulled my braid so hard I cried. I was real grateful to her, because Tang was a special treat. We only got it once a month when Mr. Hartnell brought it from home to help celebrate all the birthdays we had that month and to congratulate anyone who had lost a tooth. So while Michael Booker dripped into the garbage can, I gave Nancy what was left of my Tang, and that made her smile.

We were friends after that, even when everyone said she was a dummy and the teachers argued with Mr. Hartnell about keeping her back or sending her to another school. Mr. Hartnell said he believed in something called mainstreaming, Nancy's mom told me. But she didn't care either way—it was just easier for Nancy to go to the same school as her brothers. Even though she couldn't read or write, Nancy was real good at taking care of her brothers. Her mom said that was a gift from God. I don't know what mainstreaming is, but if it means my best friend can be in my class, I'm all for it.

Nancy had a terrible flu when she was three. Her mom says she nearly died, and that's the reason she can't read and has trouble understanding stuff. But I think sometimes that she understands things better than anyone else, because when we were walking home that day after Miss Bickerstaff cried, she said about the smartest and most true thing I'd ever heard.

"I bet Miss Bickerstaff would like to see those pandas."

I just stopped there on the sidewalk and smiled for a whole minute. It was such a great thing to say. Not that I ever thought Miss Bickerstaff would get to see the pandas or that seeing the pandas would bring her brother back. But Nancy had a way of capturing things and saying them in ways so simple that even she could understand them. And she was right. We all needed to see something great on the Eastside. With the war and the chilly old school and the weird puddles on the sidewalk, it was about time we all saw something great. I really wished someone would build a zoo on the Eastside and fill it with pandas. I really wanted to see a panda right then. Even a picture would do.

"Hey!" I said. "Let's go to the big library!"

We had a library in our school, but I'd read everything in it already. And Nancy couldn't read, so it was hard to get her excited about going to that library. But the big library was farther west into the city, where the skyscrapers gleamed in the sun and ladies wore platform heels and trim little skirts with colored tights. That was more of an adventure.

"Okay," Nancy said. "Do you have two dimes for the bus?" Nancy has trouble counting money, but somehow she knows what everything costs in coins. A quarter for this, a dime for that. Three nickels would get a steamed pork bun at Mr. Huang's.

Nancy had no idea that three nickels was fifteen cents, but despite this, she knew that ten nickels each would get us into a matinee. Not that we ever had ten nickels each. But we could dream.

That day I didn't have any coins, so we decided to walk. We had left school at three thirty, but neither my mom nor Nancy's minded if we didn't get home until just before dark. Mom made supper most nights, which she left covered with a pot lid on the table if I wasn't home on time. Nancy usually heated up a can of soup, because her brothers would have already licked the supper pot clean. Nancy didn't mind. She liked soup.

We headed west along Hastings Street, stopping to look in store windows and long for the things inside. I was hoping that Kellie Rae would be around—maybe she would give us a dime for a Popsicle—but I didn't see her. It was a long walk, and some of it was uphill, so by the time we got to the big library we were hot and thirsty. Nancy made a beeline for the water fountain. We both drank so much our bellies sloshed as we walked into the children's section.

The librarian looked up as we entered. She is a friendly librarian. She never shushes anyone unless they are being really noisy, and she lets kids lie on the floor reading comics for as long as they want. Nancy pulled out some of the puzzles and blocks they kept for little kids. She was pretty good at that sort of thing.

I went to my favorite section—nature books. I'd read just about every book they had about my three favorite animals—spiders, jellyfish and eagles. I had also read all the books about ferns and some about cacti, which were my favorite plants. I scanned the spines of the books, trailing my fingers along them, almost believing that the book I wanted might feel magically warm under my touch. But then I spotted what I was looking for—a nice fat book about pandas. I lugged it back to the soft rug where Nancy was building a tower of blocks, opened it in my lap and started to read.

It didn't take long for me to decide that pandas were now on my list of favorite animals. They have *tiny* babies and eat nothing but bamboo. They have thumbs. In Chinese, their name means "bear cat." I decided I liked them even more than jellyfish. In fact, they were so interesting and cute, I decided I liked them more than most people!

I sat there studying the book until the librarian told us the library was closing. I didn't have a library card. Mom was afraid I would lose books and she would have to pay for them. She was right in a way. I lost things all the time. Still, I was sure sad I couldn't borrow that panda book.

On the way home, we saw Kentucky Jack on Hastings Street. He had two empty bottles, one in each hand, and was swaying like a thin tree in a breeze. I figured he was about to plop over, so Nancy and I took the bottles out of his hands and gave him a little shove backward to where there was a wall for him to lean on.

"Sit down, Jack," I said. He slid down the wall and sat on the sidewalk. Real obedient Jack was, when he was drunk.

I hated to leave him like that. I knew he would throw up, and then he would smell real bad for days until one of the Salvation Army people managed to lure him into the shelter for a shower and clean clothes. But it was getting late and I was hungry. And anyway, now that Nancy and I had an empty bottle each, we could share a licorice whip. We walked along Hastings to the liquor store, where we stood outside making sad eyes at the clerk until he came out with two coins for our bottles. Then we ran around to Mr. Huang's and bought the licorice. We ate it from both ends until we were nearly kissing, and then I let Nancy have the last inch.

When I got home I could tell it was going to be a no-supper night. Mom was asleep on the couch, smelling sweet and like medicine. I made myself some toast and drank the last of the milk before going back to check on her. She opened her eyes as I sat down beside her.

"Scheherazade," she mumbled.

Four
Heather Bird Song

Mom is an alcoholic. She explained it all to me when I was little—how she's doing the steps and going to meetings and all. Once in a while she "slips," which I always want to smile about even though I know it's wrong. It's just that when Mom says she *slipped*, I always imagine her slipping on a banana peel or something and landing in a glass of wine. To be honest, I think if I ever saw someone slip on a banana peel, I wouldn't laugh. It's not polite to laugh when people hurt themselves. Miss Bickerstaff says sometimes people laugh when they're scared because that's how they deal with things. Maybe that's me.

Mom says she tries not to slip, but sometimes she can't help it. She'll be on her way home from work, and somebody she knows from the neighborhood will say, *Birdy! What's goin' on? How's it hanging? Why dontcha come have a drink with us?* Even though she's told everyone that she doesn't drink anymore, and even though she knows that with her it's never just one drink, she goes into the bar and comes out two or three hours later, stumbling and tripping back to our apartment, where she falls asleep on the sofa and wakes up with a headache.

Mostly when slips happen, it's not too scary. The good thing about Mom's slips is that once she's had one, she never has another one for months and months. Once we went a whole year. The bad thing about Mom's slips is that sometimes she doesn't come home until late, or she falls asleep before she makes supper and then she cries when she wakes up. I'd already seen Miss Bickerstaff cry that day, so I was not looking forward to seeing Mom cry too. But what could I do? I just sat there and waited.

"Scheherazade," she said again, tears coming up in her eyes. "I have some news."

I was surprised at first, until I remembered what had happened at school. "I know," I said. "Miss Bickerstaff's brother died in the war. It's real sad."

"No, honey, it's not that." She sat up on the sofa and rubbed her eyes, which looked sore and puffy. "What time is it?"

I looked at the clock. "It's eight thirty," I said. "What's the news?"

Mom looked at me real deep and long. She put her hand on my cheek, and I started to feel scared, like what she was about to tell me was going to be just awful.

"Journey," she said, "your dad's come back."

My mouth opened. It was as if someone had pulled down on my lower jaw and left it hanging there like a mailbox waiting for a letter.

"What?" I finally said.

"I saw him on Hastings Street. We had a couple of drinks together. He asked about you."

I didn't know what to say. Obviously I knew I had a father, because everyone does, even cockroaches, but he was far away from the real part of my life and always had been. I couldn't quite believe there was a man walking around somewhere near Hastings Street who was actually my real live father. Mom never talked about him and I had learned not to ask about him, so it was almost like that part of me just didn't exist. When people asked me about my father, I simply said, *I don't have one* and hoped that answer would shut them up. Now I was the one left speechless.

"Where has he been?" I finally managed.

"He was down in California for a while. Then he got busted and went to jail, I guess. Now he's out."

"What did he get busted for?"

"Protesting the war probably, or maybe…"

"What?"

"Honey, he was into a few things. I don't want you to get the wrong idea."

"Drugs?" I said. I know more about drugs than Mom thinks I do. She looked kind of sad.

"Maybe. I don't really know."

It only took a few seconds for me to realize that I didn't care what my father was into or what he had done to go to jail or why he had waited so long to come back. I wanted to meet him. It was like a cover had been taken off a hole in me that I didn't know was there—a dad-shaped hole. I felt I was teetering on the edge of that hole and that if my father didn't jump down to catch me, I would fall all the way to the bottom and be crushed. But then I wondered if he was the kind of man who could catch me. Or would he just let me fall? He barely knew me, after all. We were practically strangers.

And he left me once. He left me and Mom and never came back. Until now. I wanted to meet him, but I wasn't sure if I would hug him or punch him.

What could I do? I started to cry. At least it was a change from Mom crying.

Mom held me and rocked me, and eventually I felt a bit better.

"Is he an Arab?" I asked.

Mom looked surprised. "No, he's not an Arab. Why do you ask?"

"Why do you sometimes call me Scheherazade then? Miss Bickerstaff says that's from the *Arabian Nights*."

Mom smiled. "When you were a baby, I had an embroidered blanket someone bought in Baghdad. I wrapped you in it and used it as a sling. I took you everywhere in that sling. Jazz clubs, poetry readings, parties. People called you Princess Scheherazade."

"But why do I have black hair and dark eyes?"

"Well, your father is dark. You get it from him." She said it all matter-of-factly. As if she hadn't just told me a great and terrible secret, a shivery truth about myself, as if she hadn't handed me a puzzle piece I had been hunting down for as long as I could remember.

"Why is *he* dark, Mom?" I asked, trying to keep my voice calm.

"I suppose because he's Cuban."

"So what is his last name?"

Mom rubbed her eyes again. "Chaparro," she said. She had to repeat it a couple of times before I got it right. But finally I was able to pronounce what should have been my name.

"Chaparro," I said.

And there it was. Just like that. A new name and a new heritage. A whole new family of black curls and brown eyes and skin that tans golden brown in the summer and never freckles. Some sort of story too, I bet, like what we talk about in school. A crowded boat, maybe. A few dollars sewn into the lining of a patched coat. A trip across the ocean to an unknown destination.

Just like those pandas.

By the time I tucked Mom into bed it was after nine o'clock. Of course, I should have gone to bed too, but I knew I wouldn't be able to sleep. I wanted to find out more about my father and about Cuba, my name, my family, everything. But I couldn't leave the house, and anyway, the library was closed. All I had was what was already in our apartment, and that probably wasn't going to be much help, but it was a start.

First I tried the phone book. There was one Chaparro listed. It was too late to call. That wouldn't be polite. But I thought I could maybe call in the morning. After the phone book I didn't really know where to look. Then I remembered the *Children's Encyclopedia Omnibus* that Mom had gotten for me with coupons from cans of corn.

I looked up *Cuba* and *Cuban,* and that got me to *Havana.* And that led to *cigar* and *Spain, Spanish* and *conquistador.*

It was nearly eleven when I put the book away. I was tired and confused, which made a change from going to bed just plain tired. I had trouble getting to sleep. I couldn't stop thinking about my dad and how close he was. Twice I got up and looked out the window to the street below our apartment. There were always people wandering here and there at night on the Eastside. Some of them looked unfamiliar to me. Was one of them my dad? How would I even recognize him?

Finally I fell asleep. In the morning the doorbell woke me up. I lay in bed wondering who it could be until Mom came in, looking pale and fragile.

"Journey," she said. "Your dad is here."

Five
Tom Chaparro

He was sitting at the kitchen table, sipping coffee and reading the newspaper, when I finally got up the nerve to meet him.

I couldn't get out of bed for about ten minutes after Mom told me he was there. It was like one of those times when you wake up in the middle of the night and have to go to the bathroom, but it's dark and there's a weird noise outside and the shadows on the walls look like creepy hands reaching out to grab you. I really wanted to see him—I needed to—but I couldn't move. I pulled the covers up to my earlobes and just lay there, scared.

Then I realized I *did* need to go to the bathroom, and that just made things worse. I wriggled and crossed my legs a bit, but finally I threw off the covers, jumped out of bed and ran down the hall and into the bathroom, slamming the door behind me.

"Journey?" I heard Mom call from the hallway. "Are you okay?"

"Fine," I said as I finished my business. Then I took my time washing my hands before opening the door a crack and peeking into the hallway. When I found it clear, I bolted back into my room and slammed that door too.

"Journey?" I could hear she was losing patience. "Are you coming out?"

"I'm getting dressed," I said.

Then I didn't know what to wear! Me! I don't care about clothes. But I couldn't decide between the overalls with the patches on the knees or the faded flowery dress that was a hand-me-down from some cousin up north. It was a little short, but I had a pair of tights that only had a hole on the bottom of one foot, so he wouldn't see it. But I wasn't sure whether the green tights went with the pink-and-blue dress. So finally I decided on the overalls.

But then I couldn't decide on a shirt! I had a red one with white stripes, but the white was starting to look pretty gray and the red was starting to look kind of brown. I also had a T-shirt that said *Keep on Truckin'*, but I had no idea what that meant and was worried that if my dad asked me about the shirt, he'd think I was dumb for not knowing. Also, I thought *Keep on Truckin'* might mean something rude. Finally I thought of the tie-dyed shirts we had made at school. I didn't like mine very much, because a splotch right over my belly button looked like a corncob, and the kids at school made fun of me. But no one would see the corncob under the overalls, so I decided to try it.

My father's coffee cup was actually empty when I went into the kitchen. He was sitting there looking at me, and I looked at him and hoped so hard that he would say something, because Mom was standing by the fridge, chewing on her thumbnail.

"So," he said at last, glancing down at the newspaper. "Did you hear about these pandas?"

He took me for ice cream. Yes, ice cream, before I'd even had breakfast. It was pretty cold outside, so we ate our ice cream in the Woodwards store. A couple of clerks scowled at us, but I just scowled right back, which made my father laugh.

I wasn't sure how I felt about making him laugh. Normally I like making people laugh. I'm not the class clown or anything, but sometimes I say things that Miss Bickerstaff says are profound but that make all my classmates laugh. I tried to think of something like that to say to my father, to see if he would laugh or think it was profound. But all I could think of was *Where have you been?* and *Why did you leave us?* and *Why are you wearing an earring, like a pirate?* I didn't think any of those were funny or profound. Actually, I wasn't sure what *profound* meant. Then it popped into my head that if I wanted to, which I really didn't, I could ask my father, because he was right there walking next to me.

My father—my *father.* I was out having ice cream with my father. It was like a movie. I expected one of us to start singing and dancing at any moment. That would have turned some heads in Woodwards.

He was real handsome—tall and dark, with a big mustache—and I hoped I might run into somebody I knew so they would be curious about us. I wanted to show him off. But then again, I thought I might feel strange if someone I knew just came up and said, *Who's this guy?* Like, wouldn't that make it kind of obvious that my dad had been gone all this time? Then I worried about running into Kentucky Jack, with him smelling of barf and everything. Or Contrary Gary, who would argue with anything you said, even if it was the time of day.

Or what about Nancy, who sometimes asked strangers to read candy-bar wrappers for her and liked to try on men's shoes? She was my best friend, but sometimes she could be as weird as a three-eyed teddy bear. What would my dad think of me for having such crazy friends? I didn't want my friends to think about where my dad had been all these years, and I didn't want my dad to think I had strange friends. I was pretty confused.

Then we went into the menswear department. There were these long mirrors along one wall. As my dad and I walked toward them, I could see us both together, and it hit me. I looked exactly like him. Except for the mustache.

We also walked alike, both holding our ice cream in our right hand with our left hand in our pocket. I was wearing overalls and a tie-dyed shirt, and my dad was wearing jeans and a tie-dyed shirt. We both even had smears of chocolate ice cream on our chins, which we rubbed off in the same way, with the bony part of the back of our wrist. Only when I tried to do it, I just made the smear worse, spreading it up my cheek and over my nose.

My dad looked down at me and smiled, popping the last of his ice-cream cone into his mouth. "Here, kid, let me," he said. He pulled a red bandanna from his pocket, bent down and wiped my face. "Spit," he said when the ice cream wouldn't come off. I spit on the handkerchief and he wiped some more, leaning back to examine me.

I hoped I didn't look as weird as I felt.

"You look like my mother a little," he said. "Only less disappointed."

That made us both laugh.

Right then I started thinking of him as "Dad," not "my dad." I don't know why that made such a difference, but it did. There we were, just strolling around, looking at stuff. We talked about school and about California and about the Eastside. We didn't talk about jail or about Mom. And we talked about the pandas. "What did it say in the paper about them?" I asked.

"The usual American bu…uh, nonsense," Dad said. "There was some Chinese involvement in some incident in North Vietnam. You know about the war, right?"

"My teacher's brother just died there," I said.

"Really?" Dad said. Then he stopped and just stared at some striped turtleneck sweaters for a few seconds. I could tell he wasn't really looking at the sweaters, though, because he was frowning and looked sad. They were nice sweaters, and cheap too. "This war is terrible, just terrible," he finally said.

"What does it have to do with the pandas?" I asked.

"China might have done something bad in the war. And so the American president has to pretend he's mad at China. So now he's saying angry stuff to China, and then China says, *You know what? Scr...* I mean, *forget you. You can't have those pandas after all.* So now the Chinese are saying they're going to take the pandas back."

"What? That's awful!" I said. "Are they just going to turn the boat around?" I couldn't believe it. I knew I was never going to see those pandas, but now no one else would get to see them either. Well, except for people in China, but they had lots of pandas, and we had none. It wasn't fair. Plus, Miss Bickerstaff said that when you gave something to someone, it was wrong to take it back.

But Dad was talking again. "No, they can't turn the boat around," he said. "They needed to refuel and resupply, so they had to dock. But there's also a whole lot of other stuff on the boat that was supposed to go down to the docks in Seattle, so they have to figure out what to do about it all. The pandas are just going to have to stay where they are."

"Where are they?" I said.

Dad looked at me with surprise in his eyes. "What? You don't know? I thought that's why you were asking. They're right here, in a warehouse," he said. "Right here on the Eastside."

Six
Kentucky Jack

No one at school asked me why I had been absent the day before. We had a substitute, who barely looked up from the lesson plan, so of course she didn't care. And Mr. Hartnell was busy with some people inspecting the plumbing, which leaked and made funny noises.

It was just as well. I didn't think *I was eating ice cream with my father* was a very good excuse not to go to school. Even though it was really tasty ice cream.

Nancy had noticed I was gone, of course. Nothing slips past Nancy. She would notice an extra freckle on your nose on the first day of summer.

So when I sat next to her at recess, she said, "You weren't at school yesterday."

"Yeah, I know," I said. I was trying to act cool, but really I was burning to tell someone, and Nancy was the perfect someone. She's the only person I know who can be amazed and keep a secret at the same time. "I met my dad," I said.

Nancy just nodded. "I figured it was something big like that. I mean, you like school, don't you?"

That's Nancy. She understands *everything*. At that moment she understood that I wanted her to know but wasn't ready to talk about it. Other people would have said, *Really? What's he like? What did you do? What did he say? Where did you go? Where has he been all this time? Why hasn't he called before?* Other people wouldn't know that this last question was the one I wasn't ready to talk about. But Nancy knew not to dig too deep.

"I have a mustard sandwich for lunch," she said.

After school we decided to go see Miss Bickerstaff. She was taking time off because of her brother and all. But I wanted to tell her about my dad and the pandas, and I didn't see why that wouldn't cheer her up. Nancy wasn't so sure.

"Maybe she's still crying. Grown-ups don't like us to see them crying," she said.

I didn't think anyone could cry for that long. I mean, it had already been two days. But I still stopped in the girls' bathroom and filled my pocket with toilet paper, just in case. There's nothing worse than crying and not having anything to mop up the tears with. Your face gets all slimy and salty. It feels bad. Plus it's not pretty.

Miss Bickerstaff lived just beyond the edge of the Eastside, in a neighborhood called Grandview. And there is a grand view from up there on the hillside. You can look down onto my neighborhood, and sometimes it looks quite good, actually, not sad and dusty but tidy and sensible. That's what it's like when you look at something from far away. All the rough edges disappear.

Grandview was a bus ride from our school, and once again Nancy and I didn't have any coins. We started walking. Halfway through Chinatown, we saw Kentucky Jack begging outside Mr. Huang's.

"Jack, you better move," I said. "Mr. Huang will call the police, like last time."

"Wait until I get enough for one bottle," Jack said. It was no use arguing with him. His kind of alcoholism made Mom look like one of the nuns from *The Sound of Music*. So Nancy and I decided to help him get his money faster. That way he was less likely to be arrested. Last time Jack got arrested, he had a broken arm when they let him out.

Nancy was real good at helping Jack beg for money. She had a way of looking like a pathetic orphan, even though she was living pretty good, all things considered. She sucked in her cheeks and opened her eyes wide and stood there wringing her hands, with an expression on her face that would make a spoiled poodle cry. It was quite something.

My job was the talking. *Excuse me, mister*, I'd say. *Can you help us? My dad needs money to clean his coat. Last night on the train, this horrible man threw up on him while he was sleeping. He's come all the way from Yellowknife, where he works in the mine, just to see us. It's my birthday, see?* And so on.

It wasn't long before Jack had enough money to get his bottle. I told him to buy beer instead of whiskey so we would have enough coins left over for us to take the bus to Grandview.

"Where you goin', Sacagawea?" he asked me. I figured Sacagawea was an Indian name. Jack was always calling me Pocahontas or Minnehaha or some such thing. He was convinced I was from the rez, like his cousin's girlfriend. I hated to break it to him that I'd just learned I was half Cuban, and anyway, I still didn't want to talk about it, so I said, "We're going to see our teacher. Her brother just died in the war."

Jack cursed the war in a way that you should never curse in front of children, a real bad curse, and Nancy laughed behind her hand. Then Mr. Huang came out of the store and told us all to go away. Nancy and I left Jack with his coins and got on the bus.

Miss Bickerstaff was in her front yard when we came up her street. She was sweeping some leaves from the path and looked up at us when we got to the gate.

"Nancy, Journey? What are you doing here?" She didn't look mad or anything, just surprised.

"We wanted to come see how you are," I said.

Miss Bickerstaff set down her broom and looked down the hill, back toward the city. If you knew where to look, you could see our school from Miss Bickerstaff's yard.

"I'm okay, I think," she said.

I wasn't too happy about the *I think* part. I mean, if you have to think about it, you're not really okay, are you? It's just like in that song on the radio, "I Think I Love You." If you're thinking about it, you probably don't. So of course I was thinking Miss Bickerstaff probably wasn't okay.

All of a sudden I wanted to tell her about my dad so badly that I thought I might crack open all over the newly swept path. But I also still didn't want to talk about it. Then I realized that thinking you're okay is like being stuck between okay and not okay, because clearly that's where I was about my dad. So we talked about the pandas instead.

There was a little metal table in Miss Bickerstaff's front yard. It reminded me of one I'd seen in a movie Mom took me to in which the people spoke nothing but French. We sat down, and Miss Bickerstaff's boyfriend brought us some hot chocolate, because it was getting cold outside. Mom had told me that Miss Bickerstaff's boyfriend lives with her. I tried to be scandalized that Miss Bickerstaff was living with her boyfriend when they weren't even married. Mom said some of the parents at the school were scandalized, but no teachers want to work on the Eastside, so they didn't dare try to get her fired for it.

Actually, I'm not even sure what *scandalized* means, but I sure don't see the connection between being a good teacher and living with your boyfriend. Anyway, her boyfriend's name was Ben Wallace, and he was real handsome and made great hot chocolate that was mostly marshmallows. So I thought nothing but good things about him.

After we'd finished our hot chocolate, he played basketball with Nancy in the next-door neighbor's driveway.

"Do you know where the pandas are?" I asked Miss Bickerstaff.

"I heard they're in one of the grain terminal warehouses off Powell Street," she said.

"Wow, that's close to our apartment!" I said. "I hope they're okay in there." It seemed to me a warehouse wasn't the right place for two pandas. They needed fresh air and sunshine and crunchy bamboo to eat. "Wouldn't they be happier outside? Maybe they should let them out in Stanley Park."

Miss Bickerstaff did one of those cough-laughs you do when you don't want to hurt someone's feelings.

"Um, they can't do that, Journey," she said. "Those pandas have been in captivity a long time. They could never survive in the wild. Not here or in China. The best place for them is a good zoo."

We sat there quietly while I thought about that, and then someone, who I know must have been me, because it came out of my mouth, said, "Miss Bickerstaff, are you going to go to your brother's funcral?"

Miss Bickerstaff just looked at me. It was one of those times I wished words were cupcakes so I could just gobble them back up. That happens to me a lot. I could see Miss Bickerstaff was hurting inside, and she probably didn't want to talk about it, just like I didn't want to talk about my father. But now that the words were out, she really didn't have much choice.

"We can't go back there," she said. "We can't go back home."

"Why not?" I asked.

Miss Bickerstaff looked over at Ben, and he smiled at her as he dodged the basketball that Nancy had thrown straight at his head. "A whole bunch of reasons," she said. "My family doesn't like Ben, because, well, he's the wrong color and he doesn't want to fight in the war and we're not married…" Then she stopped. "Gosh, I'm sorry. That's too grown-up for you."

"It's okay," I said. "I know I'm only ten, but in the last few days I think I've aged about twenty years."

Then I told her all about my dad. I told her about him being Cuban and going to jail and about the ice cream and the turtleneck sweaters at the Woodwards store. I told her that he hated the war too, and that he hadn't called or written to me for practically my whole life.

Miss Bickerstaff listened and nodded. I didn't have any questions, so she didn't offer any answers. She is good like that. She knows sometimes kids just need to talk.

Sometime while I was talking, I noticed that the leaves Miss Bickerstaff had swept into a pile next to us looked familiar. I looked up at the bushes that surrounded her front yard and realized something.

We were sitting between two huge dense groves of bamboo. We were in the middle of a panda buffet.

Seven
Ben Wallace

Miss Bickerstaff said she didn't like the bamboo because it shed leaves all over her path and blocked the afternoon light into her kitchen. So her boyfriend brought over some giant garden shears and started hacking away at the hedge.

"How are we going to get the bamboo to the warehouse?" Nancy asked when we had already gathered a huge pile. Of course, I hadn't thought of that. That's another thing I do a lot—make a plan that has a beginning but no end.

"I can drive y'all down there," Ben said. I knew Ben had a big old truck. I'd seen him picking up Miss Bickerstaff from school on rainy days. His job was something to do with trees, so he needed a big truck. We started to pile the bamboo in the back, on top of his saws and axes.

It ended up being a big pile, and Miss Bickerstaff seemed pretty pleased with the way her garden looked and how much sunlight was shining in now.

"Do you want me to come with you, Journey?" she said.

"We'll manage fine," I said and climbed into Ben's truck. Nancy got in beside me. Of course, we're not allowed to take rides from strangers, but he was Miss Bickerstaff's boyfriend, and he had just made us all hot chocolate that was mostly marsh-mallows, so I figured he wasn't a stranger anymore. Anyway, his truck was real neat.

It was *old*. I think it might once have been green. Or maybe blue. Now it was gray, and parts of the metal were brown and looked like mice had nibbled at them. And the inside smelled funny. Not bad, like sweat or smoke. It smelled like cut grass and sea water and that smell you get just before it rains.

"This truck is inside out," Nancy said. I expected Ben to say, *What are y'all talking about?* but he just nodded. I nodded too. I could understand what

Nancy meant. It smelled more like outside *inside* the truck than it ever did outside on the Eastside.

Just thinking that made my head hurt a little.

We drove down to the shipyard. I had walked by the entrance a lot and gone by on the bus too, but this time we went through the gate, which, luckily, had no guard. The shipyard was huge and packed with giant warehouses, containers, empty trucks, piles of discarded crates and lots of things I had no idea about.

We drove down narrow streets and through laneways and before very long we were lost. Also, we didn't quite know what we were looking for or where we were going, so that didn't help. Ben pulled over by a gigantic tin can kind of thing.

"Is that full of soup?" Nancy said. I tried so hard not to laugh that a little tear came out of my right eye. I wiped it away quickly.

"It's probably grain," Ben said. "Or maybe fuel."

Nancy looked disappointed. She really likes soup.

We sat there thinking for a little while. Then someone asked a personal question, and yes, I admit it was me. I think because I was so confused about my own personal life and the things I did and didn't want to talk about, stuff just leaked into my mouth and came out as questions that no one wants to answer.

"Why don't you want to fight in the war?" I asked Ben. What a stupid question! But Ben didn't seem to mind. He just sighed and tapped his hand on the steering wheel.

"I've thought about it a lot, and it seems to me that this is just like when two kids you don't know are fighting in the schoolyard," he said.

"That happens at our school every day," Nancy said.

"Yeah," Ben said. "And do you interfere?"

"No way," said Nancy. "That's a good way to get kicked in the head."

"Even if one side is smaller and weaker?" Ben asked.

"Then we go and get a teacher," I said.

"And when the teacher comes, what do they do?" Ben asked. "Do they pick a side and jump in and start throwing punches?"

Nancy and I laughed. "They stop the fight," I said. "They don't make it worse."

Ben nodded. "Wars happen. The more people who join the fight, the bigger the war gets. This isn't a fight I want to join. I don't think that's the right way to help."

"So you ran away?" Nancy said.

"Grown-ups don't really run away," Ben said. "They just leave, if they have somewhere to go. Lucky for me, I could get a job here, and so could Betty."

I never knew that Miss Bickerstaff's first name was Betty. Somehow, knowing it seemed important at that moment.

"But was it hard leaving your families?" I said.

Ben just nodded and didn't say much for a good long time.

It was starting to get dark, and we still had no idea where the pandas were, so Ben tried a different strategy. He drove around the shipyard until he saw a Chinese person. Then he followed him. We did this a few times but only ended up at the edge of the water or at the exit.

Now Ben seemed like a smart guy, so he should have realized that nobody, least of all a Chinese ship worker on the Eastside, likes being followed around at dusk by someone in an old truck. I was going to say something, but I was determined to find those pandas, so I just hoped I was imagining the nervous looks we were getting. But I guess having us two girls in the truck didn't make things seem any less threatening, because before we knew it, the police arrived.

It was almost completely dark by this time, so the policeman shone his flashlight into the cab of the truck.

"Journey Song, is that you?" he said. It was Officer Pete Baker. Officer Pete comes to our class every few months to tell us not to steal, skip school or do drugs. Also, he actually caught me stealing and skipping school, but I would *never* do drugs because that's for losers. Even the people I know who *do* drugs tell me that. And the thing I stole was just gum, and Mr. Huang called Officer Pete because I cried so hard when he caught me that he was worried I wouldn't be able to get myself home without falling under a bus. And I only skipped school one time, when I couldn't find Mom after one of her slips. So all in all, Officer Pete had no reason to say what he said next.

"Journey, you're not getting into trouble again, are you?"

I was about to object when he shone his light on Ben's face. I knew that Officer Pete must have seen some things in his time as a policeman on the Eastside, and I thought he probably worked real hard at keeping his feelings from showing, but when he saw Ben in the driver's seat next to me and Nancy, his face kind of turned to ice, all white and hard and cold. And suddenly, as quick as a traffic light turning red, I knew what he was thinking.

"No!" I yelped. "This is Ben Wallace. He's our teacher's boyfriend."

Officer Pete moved one hand down and put it on his gun.

"Don't shoot us," Nancy said in a voice as tiny as a ladybug.

It was one of those terrible moments that seem to go on forever. "What's your name, son?" Officer Pete said, his voice low and serious.

"Ben Wallace, sir," Ben said. He had his hands on the top of the steering wheel.

"And how do you know these girls?"

"Like she said, sir. I'm Betty Bickerstaff's boyfriend."

Officer Pete made Nancy and me get out of the truck. Then he made Ben Wallace get out, and I begged Officer Pete not to put him in handcuffs before he made him sit in the back of the police car.

Nancy and I stood beside the police car, clinging to each other, trembling, even though we knew we hadn't done anything wrong. But there was something going on between Officer Pete and Ben, something sharp and mean, and Ben was scared. I could tell from his face. I started thinking maybe he was a criminal or something. Maybe we had been in danger taking a ride from him. I forgot all about the pandas and just wanted to go home.

After forever, Officer Pete got out of the car and came over to where Nancy and I were shivering.

"We have a little problem," he said.

Eight
Officer Pete Baker

"You see, I don't know where the pandas are either," Officer Pete said.

I nearly exploded with relief. "You're not going to arrest Ben?" I asked.

"No. Why? Do you think I should?"

Behind him, Ben was getting out of the police car.

"Bit of a misunderstanding," Officer Pete said. "Ben explained what you're doing here, and I'd like to help, but it's awfully late and you two girls should be getting home."

"But what about all this bamboo?" I said. I could still see the pile in the back of Ben's truck even in the dark.

Ben scratched his head. "I have to pick up a load of ferns tomorrow. I can't carry this around."

I thought really hard, but my brain wasn't working very well, maybe because I had been so scared a few minutes before. But then I remembered there was only one gate into the shipyard.

"What if we make a trail?" I said.

"A trail?" Officer Pete said.

"What for? What kind?" Ben said.

"Like in *Hansel and Gretel*," Nancy said. I could have kissed her. I really didn't have the energy to explain what I meant, but she said it right in one fairy tale.

Ben drove us back to the main gate and we laid out a branch of bamboo, then another a few feet away, then another and another. Finally, deep into the shipyard, we unloaded the whole pile. I hoped real hard that someone would understand and not think the bamboo was just garbage and throw it away. I hoped someone from the Chinese ship would find the trail, follow it to the bamboo pile and take the bamboo to the pandas.

I hoped most of all that the pandas would eat it and be okay.

By the time we were finished, it was real late. Officer Pete took us to a phone booth so we could call our moms. Nancy's mom said she hadn't even noticed Nancy wasn't there because her brothers had been banging pot lids all night. My mom said she was going to ground me back to the time of the dinosaurs and then make me do the dishes and the laundry for a week. I told her that was unfair and dinosaurs didn't use dishes or wear clothes anyway. So she said, "Fine! Two weeks!" Then I shut my mouth and kept it shut.

Officer Pete looked like he was trying to hide a smile when I told him what Mom said. I didn't see what was so funny about two weeks of dishes.

Then Ben Wallace called Miss Bickerstaff. From the expression on his face, I think he was facing two weeks of dishes and laundry too. He jumped in his truck and drove off, waving to us with a guilty-looking smile.

As Officer Pete drove us home, it started to rain. The streets of the Eastside look neat when it rains, all shiny and glossy, like black satin and rhinestones. But the people on the streets don't look so good. Not many people can afford umbrellas or raincoats, and some don't have homes to go to, so they just stand in the rain, hunched over like birds on branches. We saw Kentucky Jack and I thought, Well, at least the rain will wash his coat a bit—that's something.

We saw Kellie Rae. She looked real sad standing in the rain, and when she turned and saw Officer Pete's car, she moved into a doorway and out of sight. A few other people disappeared into dark corners as we passed by.

I thought it was strange. I'd walked past these people a million times, and they never ran away from me. Sometimes they said hello, and sometimes they didn't seem to see me at all. I felt sorry for Officer Pete that all the people on the street that night were afraid of him. But I guess when you're a policeman on the Eastside, that's part of your job.

I think a lot of jobs are hard on the Eastside.

"Do you like being a policeman?" I asked Officer Pete.

"Sure," he said. "Sometimes it can be tough, but I get to work outside, and I get good pay and a pension. Most people respect me."

I thought the outside part was good. My mom worked in an office all day, and she didn't like it one bit, except when it rained or snowed. Then she was grateful for being inside. I knew that good pay was important. My mom only stayed at her job because she got paid nearly three dollars an hour, which was better than what Nancy's mom made—she's a waitress and relies on tips. I didn't know what a pension was, and I didn't think it was a good time to ask. And anyway, then I started thinking about respect.

It seemed to me that a lot of people on the Eastside were afraid of Officer Pete, but I wasn't. I mean, earlier that night I'd been a little afraid, but mostly, when he came to our school I respected him.

"Can girls be policemen?" Nancy asked.

"Sure," Officer Pete said. "We need ladies on the force. They're a great help because sometimes criminals are ladies and sometimes even male crooks or witnesses will talk more to ladies than to men. You could be a cop, Nancy."

I pressed my lips together, but Nancy already knew what I didn't want to say.

"No, I don't think so," she said. "I can't read or write, and I don't think I'm ever going to learn. So I couldn't write those little notes you give people. And I couldn't fill out forms and stuff. Plus, I don't really like guns because they're too loud. But Journey would make a good policeman."

I had no idea why Nancy thought I would make a good policeman, and I didn't really want to find out, because sometimes Nancy's opinions about people are expressed by telling real embarrassing stories that I can't even believe she remembers. Like the one about the time in kindergarten when I went to school with pajamas under my dress.

I decided to change the subject.

"Is Ben Wallace in trouble?" I asked.

Officer Pete didn't answer straightaway. I didn't like that. But then he said, "Ben isn't somewhere he's supposed to be."

"You mean because he doesn't want to fight in the war?" I said.

Officer Pete parked the car outside Nancy's apartment building. He turned and looked at us. "Ben has good reasons for not wanting to fight in the war. And he's a hard worker. And he didn't lie or nothing when we talked. He told me straight out what his deal was. He's a good, honest man."

"But you didn't trust him at first," I said.

"No, I didn't, but that's because I thought…well, you never know. There are some bad people in the world who would take advantage of girls like you."

"But you realized Ben Wallace is not one of them."

"That's right."

"And you don't mind that he's a different color than Miss Bickerstaff?" I said.

"Well, when I was younger, maybe I would have," Officer Pete said. "But nowadays I think love comes in all colors and sizes, and we should be grateful for it however it looks. Though he should marry that girl. I don't approve of them not being married."

"But you're not going to tell on him?" Nancy said.

"Tell on him for what?" Officer Pete said with a grin and a wink.

"For not going in the arm—" Nancy said, but I elbowed her and she stopped. "Oooooh, I get it," she said. Then she got out of the car and ran up the stairs of her building.

"Now, Journey, I better get you home before that two weeks of dishes turns into three," Officer Pete said.

Nine
Mr. Huang

I felt weird going into Mr. Huang's the next day, what with having sort of gotten arrested the night before and all. Also I didn't have any money, and Mr. Huang hated that. He would shoo me out into the street by waving a rolled-up newspaper at me like I was a bad puppy or something. Then he would feel sorry later and give me a day-old donut. Or sometimes not. It was hard to be sure with Mr. Huang.

But I needed Mr. Huang's help. At least, I thought I needed his help. It was strange to think that I had known him my whole life, and I knew he obviously wasn't from around here, but I wasn't really sure if he was Chinese. And I needed him to be Chinese.

"Good morning, Mr. Huang," I said real politely.

"No donut today," he said, not even looking up from his newspaper. For the first time, I took a proper look at that newspaper, which was easy because for once it wasn't being waved in my face. That was definitely, probably, possibly Chinese writing on it, I told myself.

"Oh no, I don't want a donut," I said, even though I really did. But I needed something more important, so the donut-shaped emptiness in my stomach would just have to wait. "Mr. Huang, are you Chinese?" I asked.

Finally he looked up. His brown eyes were magnified by his reading glasses, so he looked a bit froggish. I kind of like frogs, so it didn't bother me. He frowned though.

"Taiwanese!" he said.

"Oh, that's too bad," I said. "I need someone who speaks Chinese."

"I speak Chinese," he said.

"I thought you said you were Taiwanese," I said.

Mr. Huang rolled those frog eyes behind his glasses. "Taiwanese speak Chinese. Why?"

I was pretty excited about my plan, so I stood up straight and tried to talk to him like a grown-up might, so he would keep listening.

"There's a Chinese boat down at the docks. You know about it?"

"I heard, yes."

"I need to speak to someone from that boat," I said. "I need to ask them about the pandas."

Mr. Huang folded up his newspaper and took off his glasses. Then he looked at me the way he looks just before he gives me a donut, kind of sad and gentle.

"That boat crew is Hong Kong. Speak Cantonese. I speak Mandarin. Different language," he said. "You understand?"

"No," I said honestly. "They're Chinese. You said you speak Chinese."

Mr. Huang sighed. "What languages do we speak in Canada?"

"English," I said. "Oh, and French?"

"Right. What about Belgium?"

I knew this from school. "Dutch and French!"

"Right. In China are many languages but two big ones. Cantonese and Mandarin. I speak one. Boat crew speaks other. Sorry." He put his glasses on and went back to his paper.

I couldn't help it. I was so disappointed that my face must have just crumpled. Mr. Huang looked up again.

He sighed. "Donut?"

"Yes," I said "I mean, no. I just want to write a note about the pandas. The ones from the boat. I want to make sure they're okay and ask if they need any more bamboo."

"Note?"

"Yes," I said, feeling the tears start to fill up my eyes. "I thought we could put it somewhere near the boat or maybe make posters of it and stick them up around the docks so they would know that we care about the pandas and want to help."

"I can write note," Mr. Huang said.

But I was really upset, so I just kept right on going. "I only want to make them understand that the pandas belong in that nice zoo in Washington, DC, and that I'm sure the president didn't mean what he said and that the war is dumb and Ben Wallace won't even fight in it and that Jack curses like anything if you even mention the war and that my dad came back to see me and I don't really even know him, but he doesn't like the war either, or turtleneck sweaters, so those pandas need a good home, not some old stinky shipyard warehouse where they're probably hungry and cold and lonely."

Mr. Huang waited patiently until I finished. Then he handed me a tissue. Then he waited while I blew my nose.

"I can write note," he finally said. "Mandarin and Cantonese are the same in writing."

"What?" I said.

"Hard to explain," Mr. Huang said. "Here, donut."

While I ate the donut, Mr. Huang got out four sheets of paper and a big black felt pen. I told him what I wanted the note to say.

"Dear crew on the ship with pandas. We need to know if the pandas are okay. Did they like the bamboo we left? Do you need more bamboo? Please don't take the pandas back to China.

They must be tired of being on a boat. They will have a good life in Washington, DC, and maybe even meet the president. If you need anything or have any news, leave a message with Mr. Huang in the corner store on Hastings Street, in the Eastside. He can't speak your language, but he can read it, which I think is pretty groovy."

"No word for *groovy*," Mr. Huang said.

"Oh, okay then. Skip that," I said.

Mr. Huang wrote the note on each of the four sheets of paper. At first I thought he was doing it wrong, because he was writing from top to bottom instead of left to right. But he told me that's how Chinese is written. There was a bit of space left at the side of the paper, so Mr. Huang went out to the back of his store and came back with a little jar of ink and a paintbrush. Then he painted a twig of bamboo down the side of each page. It was as light and delicate as a wisp of cloud and looked real nice.

I stuck three of the pages up around the docks, one near the entrance gate and one as close to the ships as I could get. I stuck the third one on the wall near where we had left the bamboo pile.

The pile was gone, which made me happy, even though I wondered if maybe the garbagemen had just hauled it away. But I hoped they hadn't.

I put the last note up on my bedroom wall, next to the picture of the spaceship landing on the moon.

I didn't think Mr. Huang would mind.

Ten
Kellie Rae

I woke up to the sound of giggling outside my window. There were always lots of weird noises outside our apartment. Sirens, of course, or coughing or crying or even fighting sometimes. I'd never heard giggling before though. It was dark still, and in between the giggles I could see weird flashes of light on the glass. So I had to get up and check it out.

I stepped into my sneakers and wrapped my blanket around my shoulders like a cape. Then I tiptoed over to my window. I don't know why I tiptoed. Maybe because checking something out in the night seems like detective work. I slid my window open and shivered as the cool night air blew in along with all the great and nasty smells of the Eastside. I could smell pork buns steaming, so I knew it must be nearly morning. I could smell stale beer and cars and, faintly, garbage that needed collecting.

Down on the street I saw another flash. I leaned out the window to get a better look. There was Kellie Rae, standing by a mailbox. She was wearing denim shorts over red tights, with high-heeled boots and a shiny silver jacket that I thought was nifty. She was smiling and giggling because someone was taking pictures of her with a flash camera.

I nearly fell out of the window when I realized it was my dad.

Next thing I knew, I was trailing that blanket down the stairs and out onto the street. I don't know why I was so eager to get out there and talk to him. Maybe I didn't like that he was taking pictures of Kellie Rae and not me. Maybe I didn't think he should be up so late. Maybe I was just mad that the giggling woke me up. Whatever the reason, I burst out onto the street and walked right up to him.

"What are you doing, Dad?" I said.

He spun around so fast that his camera swung out and nearly choked him before slamming back into his chest.

"Oof!" he said.

Kellie Rae just giggled. "What are *you* doing out here, Journey?" she said.

"Your giggling woke me up!" I snapped. It wasn't her fault. She practically lived on the street at night, and she had never woken me up before. This was all my dad's fault, and I sure wanted to let him know.

"Why are you taking pictures of Kellie Rae anyway?" I asked.

Dad was still rubbing his chest where the camera hit him. "That's what I do. It's my job," he said.

Of course, this was news to me. Up until a few days ago, all I'd known about my dad was that he wasn't around. Now all I knew was that his parents were Cuban, he'd been in jail, and he didn't like turtlenecks. So part of me wanted to hold this new truth about him, and part of me wanted to throw it back in his face.

"Well, what the heck kind of job is taking pictures in the middle of the night?"

He sighed, while behind him Kellie Rae lit a cigarette. When I scowled at her, she put it out.

"I'm a photojournalist," Dad said. "I'm thinking of putting together a piece about the, uh…ladies who, uh…work in this neighborhood."

I'm not even sure why that made me so mad. But suddenly I was madder than Kentucky Jack on a Sunday morning before the bars open. I looked at my father and saw a silly hippie who didn't know anything about anything and was pretending to be someone important. He didn't know anything about the Eastside. He didn't know anything about the people who lived here. Most of all, he didn't know that I could see through his sad little lie. He was taking pictures of Kellie Rae because he thought she was pretty. I'd spent the whole day with him, and he hadn't taken one picture of me. Which told me that he thought more of pretty "ladies" than he did about his own daughter. He was just flirting with her. And that was disgusting because I knew something about Kellie Rae that he didn't.

"Kellie Rae, how old are you?" I asked.

"Nineteen," she said too quickly.

"Kellie Rae…" I gave her my best evil eye.

She pushed her bottom lip out and slouched against the mailbox. "Okay, fifteen," she said. "Happy?"

The expression on Dad's face was worth at least a hundred ice-cream cones. He went grey as a cloud and, without saying a word, took the lens cap from his pocket and screwed it onto his camera.

"Now give her some money," I said.

Dad pulled out his wallet and handed Kellie Rae a ten-dollar bill. She grinned and tucked it into her pocket in a flash.

"Bye, Journey," she said with a wink. "Bye, Journey's dad." Then she teetered down the street in those high heels, her fringed purse swinging behind her.

Dad was just standing there with his forehead in his hand.

I was beginning to understand why Mom didn't like talking about him. I crossed my arms.

"What's a photojournalist?" I said. It came out pretty snippy, but he didn't seem to mind.

"I take pictures for newspapers and magazines and stuff."

I wanted to ask him what kind of magazines, but then I thought that if he said it was the kind with half-naked ladies in them, I would throw up on the road. "Has that always been your job?" I asked instead. That seemed safer.

"For a while, yeah."

"Was that your job when…when I was born?"

His face went soft, and he sighed. "No, Journey. I didn't have a job then. I was a student at UCLA. A freshman."

"What's a freshman?" I was asking so many questions, I'm sure he thought I was as dumb as a squirrel. If he did, he didn't let it show.

"A freshman is someone in the first year of college. University. Like, right after high school."

I had to think about that for a while. It so changed

the picture I had in my head that it felt like being dunked in cold water.

"How old were you?"

He scratched his head, looking down at me, his brown eyes sad. "I was eighteen. I turned nineteen just after…well, just after you were born."

I kept my arms crossed and hugged myself a little bit, though I tried not to let him see that. Dad just stood there waiting for me to say something. But we were getting to the part of the story where he left Mom and me, and I wasn't ready to talk about that. I wasn't sure what to think about him being only eighteen when I was born. That seemed a little young to be a father. I didn't want to say that, though, in case I got it wrong. So I decided to let my stomach speak for me.

"I'm hungry," I said.

The sun was rising, so Dad came upstairs with me. Mom poked her head into the kitchen a few minutes later, made a squeaking noise and disappeared back to her room. While I was making toast, I heard her slam the closet door about five times, then bang the window open, then bang it closed. "What do you want on your toast?" I said to my dad.

On the way up the stairs he'd shown me his press card from the newspaper to prove his story was true. I still thought he was flirting with Kellie Rae, but I decided to give him the benefit of the doubt. That's what Miss Bickerstaff says I should do when I'm not sure if someone has done something bad. Give them the benefit of the doubt. I'm not really sure what that means except that I'm not supposed to stay mad. Staying mad is bad karma, Mom says.

"Got any apricot jam?" Dad said.

And then, just like that, I almost loved him again. Apricot jam is my favorite too. I spread it so thick on the toast that I nearly needed to eat mine with a spoon. We made all kinds of slurping noises and licked our lips. Then Dad asked me if we had any coffee. I knew we did, but I didn't know how to make it. So he showed me.

Dad and me making coffee together. It made up for the fact that I'd caught him flirting with a girl on the street in the middle of the night. It was like he lived with us, like a normal family from TV or something.

"Do you want to see my room? It's really groovy," I said after we had finished making the coffee.

"Okay, sure," Dad said.

Mom glared at him as we walked down the hall and stood in my doorway, but she didn't say anything.

I showed him my closet, with the bead curtain instead of a door. I showed him the mood ring Mom bought at Goodwill that always told me I was angry. I showed him the picture of the spaceship on the moon.

"What's this one?" he asked, pointing at Mr. Huang's note.

I told him what the note said. I explained about the pandas and how I wanted to help them, how I was worried that they might be cold or hungry or lonely. When I finished, I glanced over at Mom. She looked real proud, like she wanted to say to him, *Haven't I done a good job with her?*

Dad took out his camera and snapped a few pictures of the note. Then he looked at his watch.

"I've got a meeting," he said. Then he went down on one knee so he could look me in the eye, like in a picture on a Father's Day card. That made me feel special. "I'd like to show your note to some people at the newspaper. Is that okay?" he asked.

I could barely get my answer out. The newspaper! Wow.

"Okay, Dad," I said.

Even my mom was smiling.

Eleven
Contrary Gary

The photograph of my note was printed in the newspaper the next day. Not the small, shabby newspaper that you pick up for free outside hotels, but the real newspaper, the one you buy out of boxes for a dime. I could not believe it when Dad came by before school and showed me. It wasn't on the front page or anything, but I wasn't disappointed. After all, even though the note was written in Chinese letters, I had actually made it up. So it was like having my very first story published in a newspaper! I was a real reporter at the age of ten! Like Lois Lane!

It was a perfect day.

We still had a substitute teacher at school, one I'd never met before, and when I told her I had a story in the newspaper, she told me to stop telling fibs. But even that didn't bother me, because then it was like a special secret, and special secrets are like diamond key chains that you carry around in your pocket where no one can see them.

I knew I was telling the truth. Nothing else mattered to me.

After school Nancy and I walked home, asking everyone we saw for a dime. We don't usually do this, because a couple of times we've gotten into trouble with Officer Pete about it, but I figured that day it was worth the risk. We got a dime from Kellie Rae and another one from a man she was with (after Kellie Rae slugged him in the shoulder). Then we got a dime from Kentucky Jack because we saw him being bugged by one of those church people, which he hates. We went up to him and said, "Daddy, there you are. Mommy says it's time to come home now," and so on. Then we apologized to the church lady and said we would for sure bring our old drunk dad to church so that he could find the Lord and mend his ways. Then we asked her for a dime. After she gave it to us, Jack followed us around the corner, gave us another dime and went to the bar.

Finally we ran into Contrary Gary. We hadn't seen him in some time. Mom said he probably went to the nuthouse for a while to settle down a bit. Well, I don't know what kind of nuts they're serving at that house, but poor Gary seemed worse than ever. He was arguing with a fire hydrant when we found him.

"You're not red! You're not red!" he kept saying, even though the hydrant was red as a cherry soda. I felt bad taking advantage of Gary. It's not his fault his brain doesn't work right. But I really wanted one more dime so we could have an even five.

"You sure won't give me a dime, Gary," I said real loud. "You would never give me a dime."

Gary stopped yelling at the hydrant and turned to me. "Journey Song, don't you ever tell me what I will or won't do. I will give dimes to whomever I please."

Then he gave me a dime. For good measure he gave one to Nancy too, which made her smile.

"We should have told him not to give us a dollar," she said as we left Gary and the hydrant to their discussion.

"That would have been mean. One day his head will clear up and he'll remember the people who've been mean to him."

Nancy looked worried. "Do you think he'll be mad about the two dimes?" she asked.

"We can always pay him back," I said. "By the time he gets better, we'll have jobs."

We took our six dimes to Mr. Huang's. He was stacking cans of creamed corn in a pyramid when we came in, the bell on the door jangling behind us.

"Six newspapers, please, Mr. Huang," I said proudly.

Mr. Huang looked up from his pyramid. "Why you want six newspaper?" he snapped. "You got money?" I must have looked ready to chew him out, because he couldn't keep his cranky face straight for very long. "Journey! I joke! You are famous!" He sidestepped the corn and pulled two donuts out from the shelf under the counter. "Eat," he said, then went into the back of the store.

He returned with a pile of newspapers and a tea tray. "I saved these," he said. "All day customers want newspapers. *Sold out*, I say. Nice picture, yes?" He pulled the paper open and showed us the picture on page six.

The three of us looked at the black-and-white photo for a long while. It was so groovy seeing something that I had helped make in the newspaper. And I loved that there was a little story with the picture, telling people about the pandas and their problem.

Eastside Elementary School student Journey Song composed this note with the help of local merchant Edward Huang. The note is aimed at the keepers of two pandas said to be living in political limbo in a warehouse near the Eastside neighborhood where Miss Song lives. Miss Song is concerned about the welfare of the pandas and urges the pandas' keepers to let them continue on their journey to Washington, DC, where a comfortable zoo enclosure awaits them. Details on why the pandas are being delayed are hard to come by, but it is believed that a diplomatic scuffle between China and the US is to blame.

I wasn't too sure what *limbo* or *diplomatic scuffle* meant, but I liked how the article referred to me as *Miss Song,* and I also liked how they wrote *urges the pandas' keepers* with the apostrophe *after* the *S,* because that's where it's supposed to go and no one ever gets that right.

All of a sudden Nancy started laughing. "Bear cat," she said with a snort.

"What?" I said. Nancy says strange things nearly as often as Contrary Gary does, but there was something about *bear cat* that jingled in my head.

Nancy pointed at the photograph of the Chinese note. "The pandas are called bear cats," she said. "That's funny."

"How do you know they're called bear cats?" I asked. I remembered that fact from the book on pandas I'd read at the library, but I didn't think I had told Nancy.

She pointed again. "It says right there, see? *Bear. Cat.*" Then she took a big bite out of her donut and chewed happily.

I looked at Mr. Huang. He seemed to know what I was thinking straightaway. Everyone knew Nancy couldn't read. People on the Eastside love to gossip about other people who have worse problems than they do. Mr. Huang grabbed a piece of paper and a pen and quickly jotted down some Chinese letters. He showed them to Nancy.

"What does a quick brown fox have to do with anything?" she asked.

Mr. Huang scribbled something else.

"*Don't open a shop unless you like to smile,*" Nancy read. "I do like to smile, but that's good advice for you, Mr. Huang."

I could not say anything for nearly a minute. Finally Mr. Huang rescued me.

"You can read Chinese?" he said to Nancy.

"Is that what that is?" Nancy said. "It's pictures. Each picture makes a word. That's not reading. That's just looking at pictures."

I had learned a word in school recently—*flabbergasted*. It means "overcome with surprise." I was flabbergasted. Nancy Pendleton was ten years old, and after five years of trying could not read English well enough to order from the menu at the Ovaltine Café, but she could read Chinese. If that wasn't flabbergasting I didn't know what was.

"Where in the heck did you learn to read Chinese?" I said.

Nancy shrugged. "Mrs. Chu, I guess. She babysat us until I got old enough to keep the boys under control. Remember her? She used to look at this book of fortune-telling or something. I just followed along. It wasn't that hard. I didn't know it was Chinese. I thought it was a secret code."

"Reading *is* a code, Nancy!" I yelled.

"You don't need to get all crabby with me, Journey Song," she said, looking hurt. "I know I don't know everything. I know what I know, though, and if you say that's Chinese writing, well then, gosh, I guess I know how to read Chinese."

Mr. Huang was grinning from ear to ear. "Celebrate," he said. "More donuts for everyone."

Twelve
Michael Booker

Nancy started a new reading program that Monday at school, mostly designed by me and David Schuman, who is also a good reader. We showed Nancy words and told her to ignore the letters. She said that was easy because they looked mostly like chicken footprints anyway. I didn't know how she could think English letters looked like chicken feet and Chinese letters didn't, but Nancy is pretty weird about most things, so I guessed it made a kind of sense.

We told Nancy to think of the words as pictures instead of looking at the letters. So, for example, Nancy pictured the word *cat* as a sitting cat. The *c* is the cat's curved tail; the top of the *t* is the cat's ears, et cetera. I have to admit, once I tried this with Nancy, I couldn't look at the word *cat* without seeing a cat. *Dog* was a dog lying down; *bed* was a bed with a headboard and footboard. *Foot* was a foot with only two toes. We went on like that all morning. Once Nancy had seen a word as a picture, she remembered it.

I couldn't wait for Miss Bickerstaff to come back to school so we could show her how well Nancy was doing. I didn't have to wait very long, because at lunch that day Mr. Hartnell told us Miss Bickerstaff would be back the next day. I felt great after lunch. Miss Bickerstaff was feeling well enough to come back to school. I was sure everything with the pandas would work out. Life was good. Then Michael Booker went and ruined it all.

Michael Booker comes from a bad family, so it's only partly his fault. And I don't mean a poor family. All the kids at Eastside Elementary come from poor families, and that's no excuse to be mean. But Michael's family is bad. His father went to jail for punching a policeman, and his older brother is one of those people who sell things

I'm not supposed to know about. His mother is a drinker, like mine, only she never goes to meetings and hardly ever leaves the house. She throws things too, I've heard, although I'm not supposed to gossip, so that's all I'll say about that. They live squashed up in a basement apartment on Princess Street, which is not as pretty as it sounds. Maybe Michael has more reason to be mean than most, but he had no reason at all that day to be mean to me.

We were doing long division quietly at our desks when Michael leaned over and whispered to me.

"Hey, Journey," he said, all serious-looking. "My brother found out that those pandas died."

I felt like the floor had turned to smoke and I was falling all the way to the basement.

"He did not," I said, feeling tears in the back of my eyes.

"No talking," said the substitute. She didn't even look up from her knitting.

I couldn't help it. Even though I didn't really believe him, part of me thought that it might be true. Tears started to leak out of my eyes.

"Look at the baby crying," Michael whispered. "They're just stinky bears. Nobody cares." Then he grinned to himself. "Hey, I'm a poet and I don't even know it!"

"SHUT UP!" I yelled. "You shut up and never say another thing to me ever again, you little twerp!"

The whole class stopped what they were doing. The substitute finally looked up.

"What on earth has gotten into you, Journey?" she said.

"Michael said a mean thing to me," I said, sniffing back my tears.

"Michael, is this true?"

Michael looked all innocent and said sweetly, "I was only telling her about a news story I heard that concerned her."

Well, this is where I lost control. I turned and pushed Michael and screamed, "You lying little..." And then I said a word that no child should ever say at school. It was one of those words I learned from Jack and Gary, a really bad word that sounds even worse coming out of the mouth of a ten-year-old. Some kids gasped when I said it. Even Michael looked shocked. And the substitute? She looked ready to stab me with one of those knitting needles, right there in front of everybody.

"I will not have language like that, missy. You will leave this classroom and not come back today. I will be speaking to your mother about this. Go straight to the office."

I really hate being called "missy," plus I was half-crazy with worry, so I never made it to the office. I ran out of the school, cut across the field and headed down to Hastings Street. I had to go right that minute and find out for sure that the pandas were okay and that Michael Booker was just lying about them to be mean. I thought maybe someone in the neighborhood would know something. I was only halfway to Mr. Huang's when I ran into Contrary Gary. And I mean ran into him. He was coming out of the police station, and I bowled him right over.

"Ouch!" I said, then saw it was Gary in a heap on the sidewalk. "You sure can't tell me what you're doing at the police station, Gary," I said, thinking fast.

"I will tell you whatever I want," said Gary. "It so happens I got arrested last night for creating a disturbance." He said this like he was pleased rather than ashamed of getting arrested, but Gary is contrary, after all.

"Gary, you wouldn't tell me anything you heard overnight about those pandas."

Gary got up, all proud, and dusted himself off. "Journey Song, if I knew anything at all about the pandas, I would tell the whole darn world."

Only he didn't say "darn." He said a much worse word than that, and I began to understand how he might have been disturbing last night.

"I have to go, even though you want me to stay," I said.

"Get away with you! I don't want you around!" Gary said as I ran on down the street.

I slowed a bit and tried to think. Why would Michael Booker's brother know anything about the pandas anyway? Michael Booker's brother had never done a day of proper work in his life, so why would he be anywhere near the dock warehouses where decent people made an honest living?

Michael was probably just mad at me because I can do long division better than him. And he was probably jealous because Nancy got so much attention for learning to read so quickly when he himself couldn't read until third grade. I started to think maybe I was panicking for no good reason. My mom says I do this a lot.

But then I thought about how delicate pandas must be, living in the clouds and eating nothing but bamboo. Being cooped up in a stinky warehouse couldn't be good for them. They might have caught pneumonia, and I know that can kill you because an old man in our building died of pneumonia last winter after falling asleep at night on Wreck Beach. For all I knew, the pandas could be dead—or dying, anyway—and nobody cared but me. And Nancy. And Mr. Huang. And my dad. And Mom. And okay, probably a whole bunch of other people, since the story was in the newspaper and all, but still. I felt responsible for them. I had to find out for sure that they were safe. But maybe running around in the street wasn't helping anyone.

I'd only been gone from the school for about fifteen minutes, but I started to feel kind of bad. Would they send Officer Pete out to look for me? He was the one they usually called if there was any trouble at the school. I did not want to make trouble for Officer Pete again. He had enough problems without me running around town.

Then, as I was walking past the kung-fu movie theater, thinking I should head on back to school and face the world of scolding I had coming to me, a small miracle happened. My dad walked out of the movie theater right in front of me.

Thirteen
Mr. Hartnell

"Journey?" Dad said, shading his eyes in the sun. "What...why...hold on, what time is it?" He looked at his watch. "One thirty? Shouldn't you...wait a second...what day is it?"

I was starting to think maybe anyone on earth would be more useful than my dad at that moment. He couldn't seem to get his brain to work. "It's Tuesday," I said. Then I stood on my tiptoes and tried to sniff his breath.

"I'm not drunk," he said, pointing back at the theater. "I've been at a kung-fu movie marathon." He rubbed his head.

"Well, *that's* ridiculous," I said, even though I actually thought it must have been pretty groovy.

On the inside, I couldn't stop thinking my dad was one of the coolest people on earth, but on the outside I acted like a teacher talking to a student who wasn't trying hard enough. It made me feel kind of scrambled.

Dad seemed to know what I was thinking. "You look confused, Journey. And I desperately need a coffee. Let's go."

We crossed over to the Ovaltine Café and got a booth in the back. The waitress came and took our order quickly, smiling at my dad in a way I didn't like. Then he watched as she wiggled back to the kitchen to get the coffee and a strawberry milkshake for me. I sat there thinking that maybe if she didn't wear those high-heeled shoes, she wouldn't wiggle when she walked. Also her feet would feel better. Dad lit a cigarette but put it out when I scowled at him.

"You don't like smoking, huh?" he said. "Quite the judgmental little thing. Anything else you don't like?"

"I don't like men who look at ladies like they're pictures on a wall, designed to be pretty and impress people."

Dad's eyes nearly fell out. "Wow," he said. "Where did that come from?"

"Mom's consciousness-raising group," I said. "First Tuesday of the month at our place."

"Oh God, I'm doomed," Dad said. The waitress brought our drinks. "I'm sorry I objectified you," Dad said to her. "I value you as a human being, not as a target of my oppressive, chauvinistic gaze."

The waitress slapped the bill down on the table. "Heavy," she said in a bored voice. "I hope that means I get a big tip." Then she wiggled away as I tried to fix *objectified, oppressive* and *chauvinistic* in my head.

Dad slurped his coffee with what I could tell was fake remorse on his face. I couldn't help laughing.

"Why aren't you in school, kid?" he said to me, adding about eight packets of sugar to his coffee. I added two packets to my milkshake, and he didn't even blink. I liked that.

"I got upset about the pandas," I said. Then I told him about Michael Booker and his awful family and how I swore in class and the substitute called me "missy."

"I used to ditch school a lot when I was your age," Dad said. "But we better drink up and head on back there before you get in more trouble. I'm sure the pandas are fine."

Dad left a dollar on the table. I could see from the bill that our waitress got a quarter for a tip. I didn't know if that was good or bad, and I didn't want to wait around to find out.

Dad took me straight up to the office when we got back to the school. Mrs. Bent looked up from her typing as we came in.

"Aha! There you are," she said. Then she looked at Dad suspiciously. "Who are you?"

"I'm Journey's father," he said. Mrs. Bent looked like she didn't believe him. But she looked at me again, then at him, then back to me. Finally she relaxed a bit.

"I can see the resemblance." She busily pulled a green form, a yellow form and a red form from the filing cabinet. "Mr. Song, if you are going to take your child from school during class hours, you need to let us know by filling in one of these forms." She shoved the green form into his face.

"Uh…" Dad said, taking the form.

"Meanwhile, if that child is returned to the school the same day, you need to fill out this yellow form." She gave Dad another form. "Finally, Journey has been involved in an incident where profane language was directed at another student. You will need to fill out the top part of the red form and have Mr. Hartnell sign it."

"What's the bottom part of the form for?" Dad asked.

"That's if the language is directed at a staff member," Mrs. Bent said. "Please have a seat while you complete the forms, Mr. Song. Mr. Hartnell will see you in a moment."

"Chaparro," Dad said.

"Bless you," said Mrs. Bent. I couldn't help it. I started to giggle.

"No, that's my name. Chaparro. Tom Chaparro. Not Song." Dad smiled hopefully.

Clearly Mrs. Bent was not as taken with his smile as I was. She narrowed her eyes at him and then fished out another form.

"Parental name changes go on the blue form. Bottom section."

I sat there thinking I could probably explain all this if I tried, but it was kind of entertaining, and Dad didn't seem to mind filling out all the forms. Except he didn't know my birthdate. Or what grade I was in. Or our address or phone number. I started to feel scrambled again just thinking how little he knew about me.

Mrs. Bent continued her typing, looking up at us every once in a while, a stern expression on her face. It was all an act, I knew. Even though Mrs. Bent ran a tight ship at the school, deep down she was as soft as a fresh marshmallow. But leaving the school without permission was a very serious thing, and so was cursing in class, so Mrs. Bent had to pretend to be strict and disappointed when what she really wanted was to give me a hug and make me a cup of warm milk with cookies.

Finally Mr. Hartnell poked his head out of his office.

"You can come in now, Journey," he said.

I introduced him to my dad, and they shook hands the way men do. Then they made stupid small talk, with Dad saying, "I knew a Hartnell down in Portland. Is he any relation?" and Mr. Hartnell saying, "Why, no, I don't think so. Were you working in Portland?" then acting impressed when Dad said he worked for the newspaper. This went on for what felt like an hour.

I sighed with boredom, real loud, and finally they stopped.

"Well, let me see the red form," Mr. Hartnell said.

Dad handed over the form as I sat there burning with embarrassment and a sense of injustice. I hear all about injustice at Mom's meetings.

"It's Michael Booker's fault," I said. "Ask him— he started it."

"Michael Booker lit a fire in the playground at afternoon recess. He's been sent home."

"He lit a fire?" Dad said. "Man, he must be having a really bad day."

That made me feel somewhat better. I grinned. Mr. Hartnell looked at me in that grown-up way that makes me so mad sometimes. The look says, *I understand you kids better than you know.* But I was thinking that neither Dad nor Mr. Hartnell could possibly understand me. I didn't even understand myself, and I lived inside me.

"Michael Booker's father was released from jail yesterday," Mr. Hartnell said. "From all reports he came home, packed a suitcase and got on the transcontinental train before Michael even got home from school. So I imagine Michael is a bit upset."

Boy, I hate grown-ups sometimes. Now I was feeling sorry for Michael instead of being mad at him. And why should I feel sorry for him because his dad ran off? My dad ran off before I even knew him, and okay, he came back, but still, Michael's had his dad for all these years already. Then I remembered that for some of those years Mr. Booker was in jail, so that would have been pretty hard. But then I remembered that *my* dad had been in jail too, though probably not for punching a policeman. I wrote it down in my brain to ask him about that later.

Mr. Hartnell signed the red form. "We don't need to take this any further, Mr. Chaparro. I'm sure Journey has learned her lesson and will watch her language from now on."

I sat there thinking that I would watch my language, but I did't know what lesson I learned. I was more confused than ever. Dad asked Mr. Hartnell if he could take me home even though there was still half an hour of school left. Mr. Hartnell was in the middle of answering when Mrs. Bent poked her head in.

"There's a telephone call," she said.

"Take a message, please," Mr. Hartnell said.

"No, the call is not for you," Mrs. Bent said. "It's for Journey. Someone called Mr. Huang?"

Fourteen
Jen Chow

Talking to Mr. Huang on the phone is literally like playing that game Telephone. His English is pretty good, but he has a strong accent, and his store is really noisy, being right on Hastings Street and all. So I was pretty sure that he asked me to come to the store because he had something to show me. But he could have asked me to loan him a door because he had seventeen ponies. It sounded more like the second thing, but the first thing made more sense, so that's what I went with, even though I thought it would be pretty nice to see seventeen ponies. Almost as nice as seeing two pandas.

But before I was allowed to leave school, I had to apologize to my teacher. I dreaded that. Not that I minded talking in front of the class. I'm not one of those people who is afraid to talk in front of crowds. But I was still kind of mad at the substitute. Not for any good reason. I think I was just mad at her for not being Miss Bickerstaff. My dad held my hand all the way back down to the classroom, so that made me feel a bit stronger.

The class was reading from *Charlie and the Chocolate Factory* when I got there. Books about chocolate and other foods are always popular at our school, and substitutes use them as bribes for good behavior. I guess the substitute had not had a very good day, behaviorwise. She looked up with a tired expression as I came in.

"You have something to say, Journey?" she said.

I took a deep breath. "I'm sorry for using such a bad word and making a disturbance in class. There is no excuse for something like that. In a way, I was objectifying Michael with my oppressive, judgmental gaze instead of valuing him as a human being. And, of course, you all have a right to be flabbergasted. As the old Chinese saying goes, 'Don't open a shop unless you like to smile,' which I think can teach us all something, can't it? You see, Michael just wanted to be loved, and love comes in all shapes and sizes, and we should be grateful for it however it looks. He and I just had a diplomatic scuffle and that left me in a kind of limbo. But we're all in a kind of limbo now, because Miss Bickerstaff is away—no offense, Miss. So to conclude, I'm truly sorry I scandalized you all, and I'll never do it again."

The substitute just sat there with her mouth open, her knitting suspended in front of her. The rest of the class sat like dolls on a shelf again. Then Nancy started clapping. Then Anjali clapped, and so did David. Then Jen and Patty clapped. Soon the whole class was clapping, and so were Dad and Mr. Hartnell.

I grabbed my schoolbag and jacket with one hand, and my dad's hand with the other. Then I took a deep bow and strode out of the class to the sound of my classmates cheering.

It was turning out to be a good day after all.

Mr. Huang was putting price stickers on boxes of cereal when Dad dropped me off at the store on his way to the newspaper office.

"Journey! Good to see you!" Mr. Huang said, setting the sticker gun down on the shelf. "I show you. I get it," he said and disappeared into the back of his store. While I waited, I saw Jen Chow locking up her bicycle outside. I was jealous of that bicycle, because I only have a tiny one that Mom got me when I was six. It is *way* too small for me now, so I can't ride it to school. Jen Chow's bike is cool, but it's wrong to be jealous, so I tried being happy for her instead.

"Is school out already?" I said to her when she came in.

"Uh-huh," she said. Her English was getting better and better. "Riding downhill is fast," she said. Then she picked up a basket and started putting a few things in it, noodles and cans of stuff I didn't recognize. "You were funny today," she said, inspecting a dusty can.

"Thanks," I said. Then Jen shouted something in Chinese to the back of the store. I heard Mr. Huang shout something back.

"Mr. Huang gets the Chinese newspaper for I," Jen said.

"For me," I corrected.

"Oh, you read it too?"

"No, I…never mind." I didn't have the energy to explain. "Isn't that the paper you want?" I pointed to the newspaper on the counter.

Jen looked over. "That one is Taiwanese. Very different."

"How is it different? Isn't the writing all the same?"

Jen looked at me as though I was the dumbest person she had ever met. "Writing is the same, yes. News is different." She laughed a little. "*Very* different."

Mr. Huang came back and handed Jen a newspaper. She folded it, and before she tucked it into her basket beside the cans and noodles, one of the pages flopped open and I saw something that looked very familiar.

"Wait a second. Can I see that?" I said. Jen handed me the paper. I spread it out on the counter and flipped to the page I'd seen. In the bottom corner was a photograph of my note about the pandas.

"Hallowed macaroni," Jen said. Mr. Huang said something in Chinese.

Just as Mr. Huang was about to read the article under the photograph, Nancy came into the store.

"Oh, we're reading Chinese?" she said. "Groovy. Can I help?" Then she started to read, again, like it was nothing in the world for a ten-year-old white girl with a serious reading problem to be able to read Chinese.

"Something *child wants bear cats free* is the headline," said Nancy. She pointed at the headline and said, "I don't know this word."

"*Capitalist*," supplied Mr. Huang.

"What's that?"

"Long story," said Mr. Huang as he pulled four donuts out of the cabinet.

We all chewed and sprinkled the counter with sugar as Nancy continued.

"*School child writes note...fears for bear cats. Bear cats.* That's so funny."

"Go on, please," I said.

"*Bear cats live in warehouse in…insignificant area.*"

"Insignificant area? That's not fair," said Jen.

"It means *neighborhood*," said Mr. Huang. "Keep going. Doing good."

"*Bear cats gift from center country people to beautiful country. Beautiful country bullet scold center country people.* Bullet scold? That doesn't make any sense."

"It's not *bullet scold*," Mr. Huang said. "It's *criticize*."

"Oooh," said Nancy, devouring her donut while Mr. Huang took over.

"*America falsely accused China of wrongdoing in unjust war against comrades in North Vietnam. China responded, suggesting pandas should return. However, bureaucratic,* uh, *misdeeds mean pandas must stay in warehouse. Child's note requests pandas are free. Child is not educated to understand politics…individualism…capitalist lies…oh dear…*" Mr. Huang took off his glasses and rubbed his eyes.

"Is it bad?" I asked. I wasn't sure I understood everything, but I had a suspicion that having a Chinese newspaper write about you was not good.

"It is propaganda. Understand?"

I'd never heard of propaganda, and neither had Jen or Nancy. We all shook our heads.

Mr. Huang looked sad for a minute, but then he smiled. "Never mind. Not worth the worry," he said. "I have good news. I forgot! Look." He took a piece of paper out of an envelope on the counter. On the paper was more handwritten Chinese. "Can you read it, Nancy?"

Nancy leaned forward and frowned at the note. "*Happy bear cats. Eat more Bamboo. We are waiting note from Beautiful Country. Bamboo...where.* I guess that's a question. Bamboo where?"

"It's from the boat guys!" I said. "They want to know where to get more bamboo. Oh jeez."

"At least the pandas are okay," said Jen. And I nodded, feeling like a fire had just been put out in my stomach.

At least the pandas were okay.

Fifteen
Patty Maguire

I looked up *propaganda* in the junior dictionary when I got home. This is what I found:

> *prop·a·gan·da*
> NOUN [prop-uh-gan-duh]
> 1. *information, ideas, or rumors deliberately spread widely, through media or advertising, to help or harm the reputation of a person or group such as a government or a political party*

So I figured that's what Mr. Huang meant. The article in the Chinese newspaper was trying to make me—and my country, I guess—look bad. The dictionary gave an example of propaganda that had to do with the Nazis. No one likes to be associated with the Nazis, so I wasn't too happy about that. How can wanting to help pandas be bad? Then I remembered Mr. Huang had read the words *individualism* and *capitalist*. The article had described me as a *capitalist child*. So I looked that up too. It took me a few tries to figure it out, but basically they were saying I was rich! Me, rich? I laughed so hard about it that Mom called out to see if I was dying.

Then I looked up *individualism*. It took me a while, but I finally figured out that it means when someone chooses their own path, which is what I've always been taught to do, so I don't quite know how they can think something different in China. But I guess they do.

I was pretty confused. Mom was in the kitchen making dinner, so I yelled out to her.

"Mom? What's a capitalist?"

"Someone who's not a communist!" she said. That didn't really help. Although I had heard that David Schuman's parents were communists, of all the kids in my class David is the only one who lives in a whole house, so that must mean they're rich, which means they must be capitalists, and Mom had just said…

See? This is the reason I prefer pandas to people.

Just as we finished dinner, which was hot dogs and macaroni, someone knocked on our door. I was surprised to find Patty Maguire there. Patty lives on the ground floor of our building. Her father is the building manager, and he's a good guy who doesn't get upset if we need a pipe fixed on the weekend. Patty and I don't play together that much, though, because she has two older sisters and a younger sister who take up all her time. But I like Patty. I was just surprised that she was at my door after dinner.

"Hi, Patty," I said. "What are you doing here?"

"There's a man downstairs to see you," she said, a strange expression on her face.

"You mean to see my mom?"

"No, he asked for you."

"That might be my dad," I said uncertainly. I wasn't all that thrilled about the idea of explaining the whole dad thing to Patty, given that her dad was so helpful and nice. And my dad stayed up all night watching kung-fu movies.

"Not unless your dad is a Chinese man in a suit," Patty said. "Is your dad Chinese?"

A few weeks ago I might have said, *How the heck would I know?* but, of course, I did know. "No, he's Cuban," I said.

"Well, the guy downstairs is definitely Chinese. He said he's a counselor or something. Are you coming down or not?"

I yelled to Mom that I was going to Patty's, and then I followed her down the stairs. It was four flights, with no elevator, so I had a few minutes to think.

The whole thing seemed a bit weird. Why would a Chinese man come to see me? I thought for a second that it might be one of the sailors who was taking care of the pandas, but why would he be wearing a suit? And how had he found out where I lived? Also, I knew what a counselor was—Nancy and I had to speak to one once after we saw a man nearly die in a fight outside the Astoria Hotel.

I didn't know why a counselor would be coming to see me after supper on a weeknight. I hadn't seen any bad fights recently. Now I was a bit worried.

"Hey, Patty," I said, "will you come with me to talk to him? You know, since he's a stranger?"

"Okeydokey," Patty said.

The man was standing outside the front of the building, under the awning. It was raining a little, and the awning was just big enough to keep him dry.

He turned as I opened the door. "Good evening, Miss Journey Song?" he said. "I am Mr. Cheung. How are you this evening?" He had a real strong accent, like Mr. Huang, but his English sounded pretty darn good.

"I'm fine, thank you," I said. "What can I do for you?" I'd heard Mom say that lots of times on the phone and stuff, so I thought I'd try it out. It sounded a bit silly.

"I am from the Chinese Consulate," Mr. Cheung said.

"What's a consulate?" I said.

"Do you know what an embassy is?"

"No," I said.

He looked irritated for a moment, then sighed. "I represent the Chinese government."

Behind me, Patty whistled. I turned and glared at her.

Mr. Cheung didn't even notice her. He fixed me with a serious stare and spoke firmly and clearly in that way adults do when they want to be sure you'll understand how much trouble you're in.

"The Chinese government does not appreciate children meddling in its affairs," Mr. Cheung said.

I crossed my arms. I do that when I'm trying not to look scared.

"The Chinese government is perfectly capable of caring for its property," Mr. Cheung said.

"Property? You mean the pandas? You're taking care of them now? Are they all right?"

He pressed his lips together. "The boat workers will not let us see them. Your note in the newspaper is not helping matters."

Inside, I cheered the boat workers. China had given the pandas as a gift. It was wrong for the Chinese government to take them back. But I knew this wasn't a feeling I should share with Mr. Cheung.

"I thought the note was super," Patty said suddenly.

"The opinions of children do not matter," Mr. Cheung said.

"They do in this country," Patty said. "You probably make your children work in factories and eat bugs, or you cook them in pots with noodles!"

For a moment I thought Mr. Cheung might reach out and slap Patty across the face. Even she seemed to realize that she'd gone a bit far. I did the first thing that came into my head. Mom always says to try saying something nice to someone who is mad at you.

"You speak English very well," I said.

Mr. Cheung's eyes bulged as he turned to me. "You children are clearly poorly educated and hopelessly ignorant about the world. You no doubt think Chinese people are dull, ignorant and stupid too," he said.

"I do not," I protested. "Mr. Huang is smart enough to run a store, and he's a good artist too, though he only *speaks* and reads Chinese. He's actually from Taiwan. But Jen Chow is Chinese, and she got a gold star on her report about ant hills. Plus she can multiply from one end of the school to the other, all the way up to twelve times, which is a lot harder than ten times or eleven times. Eleven times is surprisingly easy if you know the trick to it. Just like five times. But, of course, I've known the five times for ages. So has Patty here, and math isn't even her best subject. Is it, Patty?"

"No, it isn't," Patty said. "Art is. But I know the times tables up to eight pretty good."

Mr. Cheung hung his head down and pinched the bridge of his nose.

"Nevertheless," he said after a moment, "you are hereby entreated to desist in your efforts to affect the destiny of the animals in question or the diplomatic relations between our country and the United States."

His English really was good, but I didn't understand a word of that last sentence. I looked at Patty for help, but she just shrugged.

"No more notes. No more bamboo. Leave the pandas to us. We are going to retrieve them and return them to China."

"No! You can't!" I cried.

"And who is going to stop us?" Mr. Cheung said as he turned to leave. "You? A child?"

I probably should have backed down then or just ignored him and let him have the last word. Maybe I should have thought a bit more about what I said next. But Mom says I'm real bad at backing down, letting other people have the last word *and* thinking before I speak, so all in all, what happened next wasn't really a surprise.

"I might be one child," I told Mr. Cheung, "but there are at least 150 other children in my school who love pandas too. There are grown-ups all over the city who read the newspaper. And they love pandas. And I bet there are people in China too—yes, in China—who read the note in your newspaper and see it differently than you do. I bet lots of Chinese people think that the pandas were a gift given for good reasons, and that those reasons are bigger than someone having their feelings hurt about something they did or didn't do in the war. So I don't know how many people there are in China, but I think it's probably at least a million, and some of them probably don't want the pandas to be taken back. So just you wait, mister. We *will* stop you taking the pandas."

Now Mr. Cheung crossed his arms, a little smile growing on his face. "Well. I stand corrected," he said. "I certainly look forward to finding out exactly how." Then he stepped into the rain and disappeared down the dark street.

"Journey Song," Patty said after a few seconds had gone past, "you are *by far* the most interesting person I know."

Sixteen
David Schuman

When I got back up to our apartment, Mom asked what Patty and I had been doing. I told her Patty needed help with math homework.

I'm not even sure why I lied. I know you should never lie to your parents, but you should especially not lie when what you really need is someone to talk to, someone to tell you everything will be okay. And that's what moms are *for*. So it was really stupid to lie, but lies are like that. Once they leave your mouth, everything is ruined and won't be fixed for ages.

I just went to bed instead of telling Mom everything that was bothering me. And instead of falling asleep feeling snug and secure, I lay awake worrying about the Chinese government.

What ten-year-old lies awake worrying about her own government, much less one on the other side of the world? When I finally fell asleep, I dreamed I was in a zoo in China and people kept speaking to me in Chinese and feeding me donuts. Finally a giant hand came down and picked me up and threw me into a pot of noodles.

I woke up with a jolt. That's when I figured I should tell Mom about the whole mess.

I could tell from the light coming in the window that it was still pretty early. Mom sometimes started early at the office, so I hoped this was one of those days. She was in the kitchen, laying out some breakfast stuff for me.

"You're up," she said, surprised.

"I didn't sleep very well," I said. Then I told her about the man from the Chinese government. By the time I finished, her face was bright red.

"We need to find your father," she said through gritted teeth.

Mom phoned her work and told them she would be late. The whole place would fall apart if it weren't for Mom, or so she says, so they're fine with her sometimes coming in late. I got dressed and ate my breakfast while Mom made a few more phone calls. As I was pulling on my socks, I overheard her say, "Has he been staying there the whole time? Boy, I don't know what they see in him."

That last part made me feel funny. I knew Mom didn't love Dad anymore, but I had just started to love him. And I loved Mom too. No one had explained the rules about how that's supposed to work. I think I was starting to get a complex.

Mom came into my room as I was brushing my hair. "Do you have David Schuman's phone number?" she asked.

David Schuman and I sometimes do projects together because we are the best at writing. But he isn't my friend because he's a boy, and boys and girls can't be friends without everyone saying, "He's your boyfriend," and I hate that. So I didn't have his phone number. Mom had checked the phonebook, but the Schumans weren't listed.

"I know where he lives," I said.

By that time it had started raining. Mom grabbed two umbrellas and we walked out into the rain.

It was still so early that I didn't need to be at school for nearly two hours. It was pretty neat, actually, walking across the neighborhood in the early morning with my mom. We stopped at the bakery down from Mr. Huang's, and Mom bought me a pork bun. It was so fresh it melted in my mouth, like sweet and salty cotton candy.

David's family lived on the other side of our neighborhood, in a small blue house on Union Street. I knew the house because once we'd walked past it on a field trip to the ice-cream factory. David had pointed it out. I remembered it because a couple of times since then I'd walked past it on purpose to look at it again. I didn't have a crush on David or anything. I mean, he is nice and smart, but he really likes radios and spy books, and I really like bugs and pirate books, so it would never work. But I sure did have a crush on David's house.

It was like something from a storybook, right down to the white picket fence around it. Sometimes when I walked past, there was a big orange cat basking in the sun on the path. I longed to have a cat, but Mr. Maguire would never let us.

And I longed to have a yard and a path and a picket fence and a little blue house with a yellow door.

It had stopped raining by the time Mom and I got to the blue house, but the big orange cat was still curled up on the porch, looking at us in the way that cats have, as if they own the whole wide world. Mom looked at the cat for a second, then took a deep breath.

"Well, here goes," she said.

David's mom opened the yellow door. "Hi, Birdy," she said. "Long time no see. Hiya, Journey."

"Hello, Miriam. I understand Tom is here," Mom said.

"He sure is. He's downstairs. Let's go wake him up. It'll be like old times."

I didn't know what old times they were talking about, and from the look on Mom's face, I didn't want to find out. Anyway, David's mom suggested I go into the kitchen, where David was having breakfast.

David was toasting some buns with holes in them under the grill. At first I thought they were donuts, but David told me they were called bagels. He offered me one. I was about to explain that I'd already eaten a bowl of Cap'n Crunch and a pork bun, but then David got some cream cheese out of the fridge. I really love cream cheese. So I sat down and started eating breakfast number three.

"So," I said between mouthfuls. "My dad's living here?"

"Yeah," David said. "He's funny."

Just for a second I had an urge to smack the bagel right out of David's mouth—a really bad urge. It wasn't right that *my* dad was living with David, who had *his* dad living there too. And it was worse that *my* dad was making jokes and being funny with him. I might have been okay if he'd been cranky and dull. I chewed my bagel, feeling the scowl growing on my face.

"Do you have any Dr. Pepper?" I said as miserably as I could.

David didn't seem to notice my mood. "For breakfast?" he said. "Radical." But he stood up and got two glasses and a bottle from the fridge.

"How are the pandas?" David asked.

"They're about to be kidnapped by the Chinese government," I said.

"Bummer, man," David said, which made me want to smack him again.

"And the Chinese government is not very impressed with *me*."

"Double bummer," said David.

Just then my dad came up the basement stairs with our moms.

"Hey, kid," Dad said. He bent down and gave me a quick kiss on the cheek like that was nothing. I sat there hoping David wouldn't notice me blushing.

"Mom wants you to tell me about the man from the Chinese Consulate," Dad said. He sat down next to me and set a little tape recorder on the table. I waited while he pressed a couple of buttons, and then I told him everything. I could see him getting madder and madder as I spoke. Meanwhile, Mom was chewing her fingernails in the background.

"Am I in trouble?" I said.

"You're not in trouble," Dad said. "You're in the middle of something big, that's all." He looked up at Mom when he said that, and she looked back at him. Then it was as though a book opened in my mind. I could see they were thinking of me, caught between them—two people who couldn't get along even though they cared about the same thing.

"I'm sorry, Heather," Dad said suddenly.

"I'm sorry too, Tom," Mom said.

I felt like crying, but since I had already cried in front of David once that week, in class, I didn't want to do it again. So instead I asked a question.

"Will someone please explain to me what communism is?" I said.

David finished his Dr. Pepper and wiped his hands on his bell-bottom jeans. "It's a way of building a perfect society," he said. "No poverty, no hunger, no inequality."

By this time David's dad had wandered into the kitchen and poured himself a cup of black coffee. He was wearing a tie-dyed caftan and purple fuzzy slippers. "Wow, well done, son," he said. "That, like, moved me."

David grinned proudly.

"Your perfect society has been harassing my daughter," Mom said.

"Your daughter has become a tool of capitalist imperialism," David's dad said.

"She is not a darn tool!" Dad shouted. Only he didn't say *darn*. He said something much worse.

Then all the adults started arguing. Mom and Dad were both yelling, and David's parents were yelling too. The interesting thing was, Mom and Dad seemed to be on the same side. It was them against David's parents. David just looked bored. He stood up and grabbed his jacket and schoolbag.

"Come on," he said. "They'll be at it for hours."

We said goodbye to the orange cat and headed off to school.

"I'm not really sure what just happened," I said.

"It has to do with the old days," David said mysteriously. "Your parents and my parents were friends. Then your dad left, I guess, and your mom blamed it on my dad."

"Why?"

"No idea. It was the sixties."

He said this last thing sagely, as if that explained everything, but it didn't explain anything to me. As we walked on in silence, apart from David's tuneless whistling, I tried to figure it out in my head. *Why* had my dad left? Did it really have something to do with David's dad? I realized I had been assuming it was because of me. Everything—him leaving, going to jail, not ever calling or coming back—I'd thought that was all my fault. Because before I was born he was with Mom, and after I was born he left. It just made sense. But now David was saying it was *his* dad and something about communism and the sixties. I didn't even care what. It wasn't me—that's all that mattered.

It was nice to see my parents defending me together. Obviously, I knew they didn't get along. And I was beginning to understand that they believed different things. But when it came to me, they were a united force. They were both furious that the Chinese consul guy had tried to scare me. And they didn't like it when David's dad called me a tool. And they were both proud, I knew that. Proud that I'd stood up for the pandas and for the people in this neighborhood. Proud about the note to the sailors. Proud of me.

I had more than a mom and a dad. I had *parents*. And my parents were proud.

It was shaping up to be a pretty good day.

Seventeen
Anjali Singh

Anjali Singh has the longest braid of anyone in our school. Even looped double, it is still past the middle of her back. I've only ever seen it unbraided once, the day her mother came in to complain that the school had asked her to cut Anjali's hair because someone else in the class had lice. Apparently, long hair is part of Anjali's religion. I'd wished I was part of that religion after the whole lice incident, because Mom cut my hair so short that I looked like a boy until she bought some pink barrettes at Woodwards. Anjali's mom washed her hair with stinky shampoo instead and combed it until Anjali's scalp ached. So that's why she didn't have to cut it.

Anjali's dad has long hair too, which he wears under a turban like Ali Baba, only I think Ali Baba was a different religion. Anjali's dad is a repairman for the gas company. I know this because he came to our building once when the whole place started to smell like rotten eggs. It had turned out to *be* rotten eggs in an empty apartment on the third floor, but Anjali's dad didn't mind the false alarm. Mom made him a cup of tea, and they complained together about how bad our hockey team was doing, and then he left to fix a real gas leak somewhere else.

When David and I saw Anjali talking to her dad outside the school, I thought it had to be one of three things. Someone had lice again, someone had left some eggs to go bad, or there was a gas leak. When Mr. Hartnell's voice came over the outside speakers telling everyone that the school was closed for the day, and Anjali's dad said goodbye to her and went into the school carrying his toolbox, I figured out it was a gas leak, which made me pretty worried, because I had heard that gas leaks make things blow up.

Kids were cheering and screaming. Parents were moaning and looking rattled. Nancy was herding her three wild brothers back toward her home. I waved and she waved back, but she clearly had no time to talk to me because one of her brothers was halfway up a tree. Instead David and I went over to talk to Anjali, who was heading for the gate, her schoolbag over her shoulder.

"The hot-water boiler is busted," she said. "It's filling the classrooms with steam."

"Bummer," said David.

"Are you going home?" I asked Anjali.

"Yep. Mom's there, so…" She looked at me. "Your mom works, right? You can come over if you want."

I'd been to Anjali's place before. It was a large apartment over a hardware store on Clark Drive. Anjali's grandfather and uncle ran the store, and the whole family—grandparents, uncle, Anjali, her sisters and parents—all lived in the apartment together. Anjali said it had been two apartments, but they had knocked down a wall to make one big apartment, because in her culture families lived together. I told her that in my culture families barely spoke to each other, which she seemed to think was pretty weird.

Anjali's place was always fun. Her grandmother let us help her make this flat, spicy bread, and we were allowed to dress up in some of her mother's old saris, which were just super-long pieces of fabric that you wrapped around yourself like a mummy. I could barely walk in one, but Anjali looked beautiful. I thought it might be fun to go to Anjali's now. Maybe we could dress up again.

"Can I call my mom when I get there?" I asked.

"Sure," Anjali said.

We said goodbye to David as he trudged off in the direction of his house. I felt funny that he was going home to *my* dad, but I couldn't think of anything to say about it. So Anjali and I walked down toward Clark Drive, stopping to watch a train rumble into the rail yards up at the docks. I imagined one of those boxcars was full of bamboo for the pandas.

"You're worried about the pandas, aren't you?" Anjali said.

"I'm worried about everything," I admitted. "Do you think the school will blow up?"

"Dad says things only blow up in movies and in wars."

That didn't really make me feel any better. Okay, it meant the school probably wouldn't blow up, but there *was* a war on, although it was in another country. As we walked past the ice-cream factory, I thought about the last time we had been there, for a school visit. All I had cared about that day was that David had a better house than me and that I wanted two scoops, one vanilla, one strawberry. If only my life was still so simple. Now I had pandas to worry about, a dad to be confused over, a man from the Chinese government threatening me, and a school that might, but probably wouldn't, blow up.

"Hey, Journey," Anjali suddenly said. "Do you want to collect some more bamboo?"

"How? I mean, where?" I said.

"My grandfather has a truck, and he doesn't work in the store anymore. Maybe he could drive us around. Lots of people have bamboo in their yards down by the beach."

I thought it was a good idea. It was a nice day, so walking around the beach neighborhood would be fun and good exercise, which Mom is always bugging me about.

Anjali's grandfather was happy to drive us down to the beach. He sat in the truck while Anjali and I went door to door, asking people if they wanted to donate some bamboo for what we called a "school project." I didn't want to tell people about the pandas. I figured they might know about them, in which case I didn't need to tell them. And if they didn't know, they mustn't read the newspaper and that meant it was their own fault. Anyway, we couldn't waste time explaining things.

Most people let us take one or two spears of bamboo, but one lady said, "Take the whole darn lot of it. It's a menace." Then she loaned us some garden clippers and we set to. In no time at all, Anjali's grandfather's truck was full.

"To where are we taking it?" he asked in his sing-song accent. Anjali's grandfather looked a bit like a skinny, dark-skinned Santa Claus. He had a long white beard and twinkling eyes, and his hair was wrapped in a red turban. Anjali had told me once that her family doesn't have Christmas. I'd thought at the time that it was kind of sad, but having a Santa grandpa in the house pretty much made up for it.

He even stopped the truck on Fourth Avenue and bought a donut for us to share.

I directed him back to the shipyard. When we got there, I started to wonder again where we should put the bamboo. The shipyard was huge, and I wanted to make sure the pandas' keepers could find it. I was about to suggest leaving a trail from the entrance like we had before when I noticed something scrawled on a concrete wall.

"Bear cat!" I said, pointing.

"You can read Chinese?" Anjali said.

Clear as anything, the Chinese letters for *bear cat* were painted on the wall in black spray paint.

"Are they behind that gate?" I asked.

Anjali's grandfather parked the truck and got up, hoisting himself up onto a garbage can to look over the gate. He came back to the truck, shaking his head.

"That's just a vacant yard," he said.

"Darn it," I said. "Why would they write *bear cat* on the wrong yard?"

But Anjali was pointing up the road. "Journey, look!" she said.

I looked. Painted on a tall brick wall were the letters again. *Bear cat*. Anjali's grandfather started the truck, and we drove down to get a closer look. We didn't even stop before Anjali pointed again.

"There!" she said.

Every hundred feet or so, there was another *bear cat* painted on a wall or a fence—one was even on the road. We seemed to be driving in a squiggling line, but finally we got to one warehouse right down by the water. The Chinese word was written on the door, but this time it was circled.

"Oh my God," I said, even though I know it's wrong to take the Lord's name in vain. "Do you think they're really inside there?"

No one answered. We started unloading the bamboo and piling it up just outside the door of the warehouse. After we had been working for a few minutes, the door opened and a young Chinese man in overalls came out.

"Joon Yee Soong?" he said to me.

"Yes!" I said. "It's me!" Then I'm not sure how I did it, but I said the Chinese word for panda. "*Xiong mao?*"

"*Hung maau*! Yes!" he said.

"Do you speak English?" I asked.

"No. No. Okay?"

It wasn't really okay. There were a million things I wanted to say to him. And I only spoke English and a little French. But he looked so sorry that he couldn't talk to me that I just smiled. "It's okay," I said. "Can I see the pandas? See hung maau?" I pointed to my eyes and said "Hung maau" over and over.

The poor man looked miserable. "No, no," he said. Then he said a bunch of stuff in Chinese. I didn't recognize any words, and I started to wish that Jen Chow had come with us. Then I remembered that she spoke a different kind of Chinese anyway.

"I'm sorry, I don't understand," I said, looking helplessly at Anjali and her grandfather. They just shrugged.

Suddenly the man pulled a pencil out of his pocket and began to draw on the white door behind him. In moments there was a very good drawing of a man in a suit. The young man pointed at his drawing and said something, then opened the door and pointed inside the warehouse.

"That man is inside?" I said. "Who is he?" When I stepped forward to take a closer look at the drawing, I thought that this young man should probably change jobs from ship worker to portrait artist, because close up there was no mistaking the person he had drawn.

It was Mr. Cheung, the man from the Chinese government. He was inside the warehouse with the pandas.

Eighteen
Mrs. Bent

I didn't sleep that night. I couldn't stop thinking about Mr. Cheung and the pandas. I didn't think Mr. Cheung would hurt them or anything, but I thought it was terrible that he was in there with them, even though the boat crew obviously wanted to keep those pandas right where they were rather than let Mr. Cheung take them. Would Mr. Cheung convince them to let him take the pandas back to China? I couldn't stomach that idea. It would mean another long boat trip, and then what? Did China have a nice zoo for them?

After three hours of lying awake, I finally got up and crawled into bed with my mom. I tried to be quiet, but she was awake. She rolled over and turned on her lamp.

"Nightmare?"

"I can't sleep." I told her all my fears about the pandas and Mr. Cheung. "I just feel so helpless," I said. Then I started to cry. I cried for the pandas and for Michael Booker and Nancy. I cried because Anjali had her whole family living with her and because Jen Chow had a new bike. I cried for Kellie Rae and Contrary Gary and Kentucky Jack because it was raining outside and I knew they would be cold. I cried because Patty Maguire never played with me. I cried for all the times Mr. Huang had been snippy with me and wouldn't give me a donut. I cried because David Schuman got to live with my dad. I cried for poor Miss Bickerstaff, who had lost her brother, and for Ben Wallace, who'd had to leave his family. I cried for Officer Pete because people were scared of him. I cried for Mr. Hartnell, who was trying to run a school with a broken boiler and not enough books. And I cried for Mrs. Bent, poor Mrs. Bent, who had fallen to the floor with

Miss Bickerstaff that terrible day. My knees hurt just thinking about it.

"There's too much sadness in the world," I finally managed to say. Mom held me tight and whispered in my ear.

"Sadness is the price we pay for love, Journey."

"A lot of people love those pandas, don't they?" I said.

"Of course they do," Mom said.

I felt real peaceful, hearing her say that. Mom seemed peaceful too. And I thought maybe wars and fights and scuffles are the things that make it hard to talk about stuff. Maybe it's only after those things are over that you start being able to figure things out. It was one of those thoughts you get in the dark that seems to make perfect sense.

"Mom," I whispered. "Why did Dad leave us?"

She was quiet for a while. "It wasn't because he didn't love you," she said.

"Okay."

There was another silence. Mom looked up at the ceiling before speaking again. "People do stupid things when they're young."

I thought she might say more. And at first I wanted her to. But then I realized that was a pretty good answer. He was young and stupid. I could relate to that. I was young too, and I did stupid things all the time.

I fell asleep with Mom's arms around me, her voice singing softly in my ear.

In the morning, before I went to school, I asked Mom if I could call Dad. She looked hurt and a little scared for a minute, but then she gave me a piece of paper with a phone number on it. I dialed the phone, stretching the cord out as long as it could go, which was into the bathroom. I closed the door.

David answered the phone. "Hey, Journey," he said. "I'll get Tom."

MR. CHAPARRO TO YOU! I wanted to yell, but I rolled my tongue into a ball and said nothing. Dad came on the line a few seconds later.

"Journey? What's up?"

"Can you come to the school with your camera today?" I said. "There's something I want to do, and I want the newspaper to know about it. Can you be there at ten?"

"Count on me, kid," Dad said.

I left for school early. Mom saw me off with a worried expression on her face, but that was nothing new.

"Eleven o'clock?" she asked.

"Eleven o'clock," I said.

Out on our street, I found Contrary Gary putting dimes into an empty newspaper box. "Isn't that a waste of money, Gary?" I asked.

"Keeping money is a waste, Journey. Money eats at you like a swarm of biting fish, until there's nothing left. This way the newspaper people have to deal with it."

I didn't really know how to make sense of that, so I decided to change the subject. "Gary, you should not be down at the shipyard at eleven."

"I go where I please, and you can't stop me," Gary said.

I left him to his dimes and continued down the street. Outside the Salvation Army I found Kentucky Jack, all clean and shiny like he had been scrubbed with a scouring pad.

"Wow, Jack, you look great," I said.

"Well, thank you, Journey," Jack said. "I woke up looking like this. I'm not sure what happened."

I smiled to myself, knowing that the Salvation Army people must have found him passed out in the night and bathed him and washed his clothes when he was too drunk to notice.

"Jack, can you come to the shipyard at eleven o'clock?" I asked.

"Will drinks be served?" Jack said.

"Well, no," I said. "But maybe someone might give you a quarter."

"I'll be there."

Kellie Rae was harder to find. She was usually only out in the afternoon or at night, and I had no idea where she lived. I stopped in at Mr. Huang's and asked him if he knew where she was.

"She not here!" he snapped. "She bad girl!"

I got real mad at him then, for no reason other than he was being stupid and unfair. "Mr. Huang, why don't you stop pretending that you can't speak proper English and also grow a little Christian understanding? Kellie Rae can't help who she is. Mom says she's just a good girl in a bad situation."

Mr. Huang blinked. "I'm not a Christian," he said.

"You're not?" I asked.

"No. Buddhist," he said.

"And how do Buddhists feel about judging people?"

He looked ashamed then. "Bad," he admitted. "Here, have a donut."

I took the donut. "If you see Kellie Rae this morning, you tell her to come to the shipyard at eleven. You come too," I said sternly. "And bring more donuts."

It was getting late, and I had to get to school. I ran down Hastings Street, blending in with the crowds of kids heading up the block to our school. When I got there, my dad was already in the schoolyard, talking to Mr. Hartnell.

"You're early," I said, interrupting them.

"Mr. Hartnell here said he'd take me around the school to get some pictures. Broken water heaters and crumbling plaster and such."

"We have plenty of that," I said. "Can I talk to Mr. Hartnell privately?"

Dad wandered off to take pictures of a swing that was hanging by one chain. Mr. Hartnell turned to me.

"What do you want to talk about, Journey?"

"Is Miss Bickerstaff here today?" I asked.

"Yes, she is. It's her first day back."

"Is she sad?"

Mr. Hartnell got one of those looks, like he couldn't quite believe someone had just come out and asked that. But I knew I had asked the right question, because he gave a great big sigh and put his hands in the pockets of his slacks.

"She's sad, yes. But she'll get better slowly. You shouldn't worry yourself about that, Journey."

Mom says I "size people up" sometimes. I look at them as though I'm deciding whether to trust them. Mom says I do it all the time, so much that her friends laugh about it. I knew at that moment that I was sizing Mr. Hartnell up. Was he going to go along with what I had planned? Was he on my team? I only had one way to find out.

"Mr. Hartnell, if there was a way you could make Miss Bickerstaff happy for just a little while, I mean *really* happy, would you do it?"

He thought about it for a moment. "Why, yes, Journey," he said finally. "I believe I would."

I was done sizing him up. So that's when I let Mr. Hartnell in on my plan.

At ten o'clock I went to the office with a piece of paper, a cameraman from the TV station and my dad. Mrs. Bent was waiting for me.

"I'm so proud of you, Journey," she said. She leaned back and got the microphone for the announcements, put it on her desk in front of her, then turned it so it was facing me. Beside me I heard the cameraman turn his camera and tape recorder on. Dad took out his own camera and started snapping some pictures.

Mrs. Bent clicked something on the microphone. There was a loud buzzing noise and everything in the school went silent. I took out my piece of paper and started to read.

"Good morning, teachers, guests and boys and girls." I had to gulp then, because I was so nervous, but Dad took a picture of me and gave me a thumbs-up, so I kept going. "Today we would like to welcome back Miss Bickerstaff. For those of you who don't know, she has been away because her brother died in the war and she was feeling too sad to teach. Miss Bickerstaff loves teaching, so if she was too sad to teach, then that means she was very, very sad."

Mrs. Bent dabbed her eyes. I drew a big breath and read on. "This war is making lots of people sad, it seems, and there's a whole lot of other stuff too that makes people sad. Some people don't have enough to eat, or anywhere nice to live." I thought about Kellie Rae and Gary and Jack. "Some people live far away from their country and have a hard time understanding the way we talk." I thought about Jen Chow and Mr. Huang. "Some people's families are mixed up or messed up or missing people or just weird." I thought about Michael Booker and

David Schuman. And I thought about myself and my dad, who I had just met. "And some people just have a hard time doing things that the rest of us can do real easy." I thought of Nancy. "Some people have real hard jobs." I thought of Anjali's dad and Patty Maguire's dad. "Some people just try really hard to keep going, even though life seems to make things hard for them. They have to make hard decisions and try every day not to make mistakes." I thought of Mom and Miss Bickerstaff and Ben Wallace. And I thought of Officer Pete, because he *did* have a real hard job, and a policeman can't afford to make mistakes, no matter what. "Some people are sad because it seems that no matter what they do, nothing ever gets better." I looked up at Mrs. Bent, who had tears streaming down her face by this time, and Mr. Hartnell behind her, who was staring at a stain on the carpet.

"The thing is, we can make each other happy, if we try. We don't have to be mean to each other. We can help each other. We could be more like animals in a way, not less. Because there is a perfect animal in the world who only wants bamboo to eat and somewhere comfortable to sleep. That's what makes them happy. And we can help them today. They need our help. And I believe that helping them will make us happy—I know it will make me happy. And I think it will make Miss Bickerstaff happy. So I, Journey Wind Song Flanagan Chaparro, am asking you to come with me to the shipyard. We don't have any parental permission, and we don't have any buses, but it's not raining and we'll all be together, so if you want to come, then let's meet in the schoolyard and go help our friends find their way to their new home." I finished with a sigh. It felt right. Mrs. Bent clicked off the microphone. Then she blew her nose into a lacy hanky.

The cameraman turned his camera off and looked at my dad. "I'm going to get an award for this," he said.

Nineteen
Mr. Cheung

We arrived at the shipyard just before eleven, like I'd planned. The younger kids were tied together with long strings looped around their wrists. Some of the older kids had wandered into people's yards, thrown chestnuts at each other and made faces at passing cars, but we'd all gotten there in one piece. Soon there were a hundred kids and nearly as many adults, all gathered outside the warehouse. Gary and Jack were there, and even Kellie Rae. I stood there holding Miss Bickerstaff's hand and wondering what to do next. As usual, I hadn't quite completed my plan before going ahead and putting it to work.

The warehouse door was closed and locked in front of me, like some magical gate to a forbidden castle. The Chinese word for *panda* could still be seen, clear as anything. But someone had crossed out the drawing of Mr. Cheung with red spray paint. Did that mean he was gone? I didn't have to wait long to find out.

The door opened and Mr. Cheung came out. He had an expression on his face like someone who has just drunk a gallon of vinegar.

"Journey Song," he said to me, only he made it sound like a swearword.

"Mr. Cheung," I said right back, hoping for the same effect.

"I should have all of you arrested for trespassing."

I pointed to Officer Pete, who had been waiting for us when we arrived. "There's a policeman right over there. Why don't you go tell him to arrest us?"

Officer Pete gave me a big grin and a smile. Mr. Cheung glared at me.

"Let me tell you about my day, Miss Song," he said. His lips were pulled so tight I thought they might split apart. "This morning at 2 AM I received a call from my government. Then I received a call from the president's office in Washington at 3 AM.

At 4 AM my mother called and told me I was bringing shame on my whole family and our ancestors. Then at 5 AM my daughter had a nightmare that woke up the entire house. At 6 AM my daughter's nanny told me she would not make my daughter's breakfast unless I agreed to let the pandas go to Washington. At 6:30 I fired her. At 6:45 my wife said she would divorce me if I fired the nanny. At 7 AM I rehired the nanny and had to raise her wages. At 7:30 my government called again. I told them to call the president's office directly, as I was going back to bed." Mr. Cheung crossed his arms and sighed.

Everyone, including Mr. Cheung, seemed to be waiting for me to say something. I said the first thing I could think of. "What have you learned, Mr. Cheung?" That was something both Mom and my teachers said when something went wrong or I was having a bad day.

"What?" Mr. Cheung looked very, very tired. I decided to help him out.

"Well, I think maybe you've learned that there are a lot of people in the world who are affected by the decisions you or your government makes. Not just people, but pandas too. I hope your government learned that too. And the president in Washington and everyone who works for him. Also, you probably weren't paying your nanny enough to begin with."

Beside me, Miss Bickerstaff gave a little snort of laughter, which she covered with her hand.

Mr. Cheung pinched the top of his nose. "What are you doing here, Miss Song?"

"We came to make sure the pandas don't get sent back to China, because—"

"The pandas are not being sent back to China," Mr. Cheung said, but as usual I just kept on talking.

"—I'm worried that they won't survive the journey, because that would be very hard for them. They've been locked up in the warehouse for ages, and they normally live up in the clouds, and we've been bringing them bamboo and everything, but I'm not sure if that's enough for them, and, well, it would just be a tragedy if anything were to happen to them. A tragedy. So, in conclusion—"

"THE PANDAS ARE NOT GOING BACK TO CHINA!" Mr. Cheung yelled.

Everyone got so silent that you could have heard a seagull wing flapping clear across the harbor.

If it had been nighttime, we would have heard crickets, I'm sure.

"What?" I said.

"The pandas aren't going back to China!" Nancy yelled before Mr. Cheung could repeat himself.

Everyone started to cheer. Nancy turned around and held her arms up in victory, as though everyone was cheering for her. Then, toward the back of the crowd, I saw Kellie Rae hold her arms up. People turned to her and cheered again. Then Michael Booker held his arms up, and so did Contrary Gary and Ben Wallace and Anjali's grandfather and Jen Chow. Soon we all had our arms in the air and were cheering for each other.

"We did it!" Nancy shouted to me. I wasn't sure how we'd done it, and maybe it would have happened anyway, but everyone there felt that triumph as much as I did. We mattered in that moment. To each other and to the world. We were important. We had changed the course of history—or at least the course of the lives of those pandas. And that mattered. That mattered a lot.

Gradually the cheering stopped and changed into just the murmur of a lot of people talking to each other, excited but not loud. I turned to Mr. Cheung, who had a strange expression on his face. He didn't seem happy. He didn't seem mad. He seemed like someone who didn't like his job anymore.

"You can go now, Miss Song. You got what you wanted."

The grin fell off my face like a baby bird out of its nest.

"Go? What about the pandas?" I said.

"What about them?" Mr. Cheung said. "We are taking them to the airport this evening. The zoo is sending a special plane."

I suppose I should have been happy. It was almost everything I had hoped for. Almost. But I felt kind of empty inside. And everyone got really quiet, when they should have been cheering. It wasn't until I turned to Miss Bickerstaff that I remembered she was the reason I had wanted to help the pandas in the first place. I had wanted to make her happy. And I didn't know if she was.

"Are you happy?" I asked her.

"Of course I am, Journey. I'm very happy."

But she didn't look happy. She looked far away. Ben Wallace put his arm around her shoulder. I saw a couple of parents and other grown-ups look in their direction with pinched-up mouths. I wanted to shout at them that love comes in all shapes and colors, but I didn't think that would help.

Everyone stood there quietly until Mr. Cheung finally spoke again.

"Well?"

But before I could answer, the boat worker that I had met before came out through the door.

"Hello! Joon Yee!" He came and shook my hand so hard my whole body jiggled. "See pandas now?"

My heart flickered. "See them?" I said. "Really?"

He and Mr. Cheung started to argue. And if you think arguments in English are hard to follow, you should hear two people arguing in two kinds of Chinese. I turned to Mr. Huang and Jen Chow to see if they could understand what was going on, but they both just frowned. Finally Mr. Cheung threw his hands up in frustration, yelled something and stomped back through the door.

The boat worker looked disappointed. "Only you and two, Joon Yee," he said.

I didn't understand him at first, but Miss Bickerstaff explained, "He's saying that you can see the pandas, Journey. But you can only bring two friends."

Only two friends? How could I decide? Of course Nancy was my best friend, but I'd been hanging around with Anjali a lot too. And she and her grandpa had helped with the bamboo and all. What about Mom or Dad? Could I choose one but not the other? And what if I chose both of them? Would they fight the whole time?

Then I remembered Miss Bickerstaff again. I remembered thinking that her seeing the pandas would make her happy again. Wasn't she an obvious choice? So I could take her and Ben Wallace with me. But then I thought of poor Kellie Rae and her terrible life. And Contrary Gary and Kentucky Jack—but if I took them to see the pandas, would they even remember the next day? What about Mr. Huang? Without him I never would have been able to get the note to the boat workers. It never would have been in the paper here and in China. Surely he should see the pandas too. In fact, everyone here deserved to see the pandas as much as I did. I was about to explode in a puff of not being able to decide when Nancy solved everything for me.

"Why don't you take the guy with the TV camera in?" she asked. "Then we can all watch later."

It was, as usual, a brilliant idea. So a few minutes later, Miss Bickerstaff, the cameraman (whose name was Brad) and I were ready to go into the warehouse to see the pandas. Just before we went in, my dad stopped me and slipped his fancy camera around my neck. "Turn this to focus, and press this to take a picture, okay? I just reloaded it, so there are over forty shots in there. Use the whole roll if you have to. Brad, can you set the f-stop for her?"

I had no idea what that meant, but Brad seemed to, so I decided not to worry. The boat worker held the door open for us, and we went inside.

Twenty
Journey Wind Song Flanagan Chaparro

We were in a long, dark hallway. Well, it would have been dark if the camera guy, Brad, hadn't turned on this real bright light that lit the way for us like headlights on a car. Mr. Cheung turned and made a face at him.

"You won't need the light when we get to the pandas. The room is well lit."

"Groovy," Brad said. Mr. Cheung just scowled. Next to me, Miss Bickerstaff squeezed my hand.

We turned a corner. The boat worker waved at us, a big grin on his face. He headed down another long hallway, only this one had high dirty windows all along one side. Despite the dirt, they filled the hallway with light, and Brad flicked his light off.

I checked Dad's camera, reminding myself, Focus with this, take a picture with this, focus with this...

I don't know why I was nervous. It's not like pandas are dangerous. Anyway, Miss Bickerstaff would never let anything bad happen to me. And Brad would be filming them, so everyone would get a good look. Any photographs I took were just going to be extras. But then I remembered—my dad worked for the newspaper! Could a picture I took be in the newspaper? People were pretty interested in the pandas. Maybe a photo would be on the front page. Maybe my name would be under the photograph, the way Dad's name was.

I started to wonder what name I would use. Would I use Journey Song because that's how most people knew me? Or would I use Journey Flanagan, because that was on my birth certificate? Maybe I could use Journey Chaparro, because kids usually had their dad's last name. Only Journey Chaparro sounded a bit like a superhero's girlfriend or something. I would have to decide, but I couldn't decide just then. I thought I might talk to Miss Bickerstaff about it later. She would know what to do.

Turning to look up at her, I saw she had a kind of strange expression on her face, like she was walking through a dream. She wasn't exactly smiling, but she didn't look sad. She looked peaceful. I decided that peaceful was the best way for her to look. I squeezed her hand, and she glanced down at me and winked.

The boat worker opened a door. We stepped through into a large open space. There were high windows all around us, shining light down onto the concrete floor. At the back of the huge room, some wide doors were open to the dock and the water beyond. Sunlight and fresh air were streaming in. And in the middle of some crates and boxes and other mess was an enclosure made of chicken wire and two-by-fours, lined with bamboo and newspaper. And in the middle of that were the pandas.

I never thought I would see anything more beautiful than the studded denim jacket Nancy and I once saw in the store window at Woodwards, but these pandas made that jacket look like an old dishrag.

One of the pandas was lying on its back with its four paws wiggling in the air, and the other was sitting, just like a person, with a sprig of bamboo in its fist, chewing on it the way a person might chew on a toothpick. They looked up at us as we came in. Next to me I heard Brad start his camera. It whirred and clicked, but I could barely hear it over the pounding of my heart.

The pandas were just lovely. So beautiful I felt like I was going to cry. I blinked and blinked until finally I remembered the camera around my neck. I lifted it up and turned the lens to focus it. Through the lens I saw the pandas both look at me, like they were posing.

But it was more than that. It was like they were speaking to me. *Thank you*, they said. *Thank you for caring. Not just about us, but about the world and everyone in it.* I snapped a picture and hoped that somehow what they were saying would come through on film.

Beside me I heard Miss Bickerstaff sniff. She was crying! But it wasn't like the crying on that awful day she learned her brother had died in the war. It was like the way Mom cried when she got a raise at work that meant we could get the bigger apartment.

They were tears not just of happiness, but of something deep and wonderful. They were tears of understanding something for the first time in your life. I knew all about what kind of tears they were, because I was crying them too.

The pandas just watched us. Thoughtfully, like they understood.

Later, when Dad told me that Brad had filmed for over half an hour, I couldn't believe it. Had we been in there that long? It had felt like only a minute or two. They got a friend of theirs to rush the processing of the film, and we showed it in the gym at school two days later.

I watched that film with the rest of my school and all the people from the neighborhood, and I felt goose bumps rise on me as the me in the film looked back at the pandas. I wiped my eyes in the film. I wiped my eyes in the gym. Something amazing had happened. No one, not one of us, would ever forget it.

No one spoke, in the film or in the gym. The pandas sat and looked back at us, chewed bamboo and eventually curled up and went to sleep, like they were trying to show us how to really live the good life. It was the best movie I had ever seen. Better than *Pippi Longstocking*.

I thought so many thoughts as I watched the film that I wondered if my brain might just explode. I thought about my friends and my family. I thought about Miss Bickerstaff and the school and the war and China and the pandas. I had a wonderful daydream about how the world might be from now on. How the school might be better, how Miss Bickerstaff and Ben Wallace would get married and no one would care about what color they were. I thought about Nancy becoming a great writer or poet, and Anjali taking over her family's business and making it grand and huge. I thought about Michael Booker and how one day he would forget his terrible family and become a good man with a good job—maybe a policeman, like Officer Pete. I thought about Jen Chow and Mr. Huang practicing their English together. I thought I would try to make better friends with Patty Maguire, because she was probably sick of her sisters by now, and we did just live upstairs. I thought of David Schuman and how I would ask him if I could pat his cat one day and maybe get some ice cream together.

I thought about Kentucky Jack going to meetings with my mom and giving up the drink for real, and Contrary Gary getting his head fixed. I thought about poor Kellie Rae and decided to give her all the dimes in my piggy bank so she could call her family and ask them to come rescue her.

I thought about my mom and dad and how I wished they would love each other again and that we could be a family. I knew that wasn't going to happen, but it was nice to think about.

Mostly I thought about the pandas, and how they were going to have a new home in Washington, and how happy they were going to make people there. I knew that's all they wanted from life—to make people happy. Then I knew for sure that was all I wanted too. I had made people happy, just like I'd wanted to. I had turned people's eyes away from the puddles and the steamy school and the smell of

Jack's coat and the dirt and the poverty. I had made them look at each other instead and see friends. I had let them see the pandas and see beauty.

I had changed the world. Me. Journey Wind Song Flanagan Chaparro had changed the world.

With all the help I had, it didn't even seem that hard.

Author's Note

In 1972 the government of China gifted two giant pandas, Ling-Ling and Hsing-Hsing, to the people of the United States in a friendly gesture that has come to be known as "Panda Diplomacy." Ling-Ling and Hsing-Hsing lived long, lazy panda lives in their enclosure at the National Zoo in Washington, DC, and their playful antics were enjoyed by many millions of visitors. Since then China has given or loaned pandas to zoos in countries all over the world, strengthening their ties with those countries as well as establishing giant pandas as ambassadors for China and the wildlife-preservation movement.

The relationship between the US and China in 1972 was somewhat fraught, the US embroiled in the Vietnam War, and China deeply entrenched in communism and anti-American sentiment. Despite that, the gift of Ling-Ling and Hsing-Hsing and their arrival in the US went off without incident.

This book imagines a "what-if" situation in which the pandas' journey was not quite so smooth.

Acknowledgments

First, I would like to thank the people of the Downtown Eastside in Vancouver, British Columbia, for always retaining their pride in the face of criticism and scorn. Like all lower-income downtown neighborhoods throughout the world, the DTES has its share of problems. But it also has a rich history and a diverse population of artists, business owners, families, new arrivals, students and professionals. I hope that in spinning this little yarn, I will help readers see this part of the world and all urban "slums" in a gentler, more understanding light.

Thanks to Kris and Carolyn for believing in this book and to Sarah for once again being an editor who gets me. I couldn't have written this book without the support of my husband, Len, who works in the DTES every day and rarely complains, and my daughter, Lucy, who is turning out to be a great little beta reader.

Finally, thanks to Ling-Ling and Hsing-Hsing, two pandas who probably never knew how important they were.

Gabrielle Prendergast wrote her first book in crayon at the age of about four and has seldom stopped making up stories since. She is the author of two YA verse novels, *Audacious* and *Capricious*, and *Frail Days* in the Orca Limelights series. She lives in Vancouver, British Columbia, with her husband and daughter.

WHAT TO READ NEXT...

"Terrific."
—*Kirkus Reviews*

"Compelling...
a page-turner."
—*Booklist*

9781459808348 PB

*How do you plan for the future when your own
parents don't believe you have one?*

Wolf's mother is obsessed with saving the world's
honeybees, so it's not too surprising when she
announces that she's taking her Save the Bees show
on the road—with the whole family. Wolf thinks
it's a terrible plan, and not just because he'll have
to wear a bee costume—in public.

9781459808720 PB

Janelle was the one in the accident.
So why is it Dana who's hurting?

Best friends Dana and Janelle had big plans for grade six. Run on the cross-country team together. Try out for volleyball. They'd even planned to be partners for their class project. Neither girl could have known that a biking accident would land Janelle in the hospital and change everything.

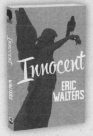